A GANGSTA'S EMPIRE

Lock Down Publications & Ca$h Presents

A Gangsta's Empire
By Tranay Adams

.

Lock Down Publications
P.O. Box 870494
Mesquite, Tx 75187

Visit our website at **www.lockdownpublications.com**

First Edition December 2018
Printed in the United States of America
This is a work of fiction. Names, characters, places, and incidents either are products of the author's imagination or are used fictitiously. Any similarity to actual events or locales or persons, living or dead, is entirely coincidental.

Cover design and layout by: Dynasty's Cover Me
Book interior design by: Shawn Walker
Edited by: Shon Progue

Stay Connected with Us!

Text **LOCKDOWN** to 22828 to stay up-to-date with new releases, sneak peaks, contests and more…

Thank you!

Submission Guideline.

Submit the first three chapters of your completed manuscript to ldpsubmissions@gmail.com, subject line: Your book's title. The manuscript must be in a .doc file and sent as an attachment. Document should be in Times New Roman, double spaced and in size 12 font. Also, provide your synopsis and full contact information. If sending multiple submissions, they must each be in a separate email.

Have a story but no way to send it electronically? You can still submit to LDP/Ca$h Presents. Send in the first three chapters, written or typed, of your completed manuscript to:

LDP: Submissions Dept
Po Box 870494
Mesquite, Tx 75187

DO NOT send original manuscript. Must be a duplicate.

Provide your synopsis and a cover letter containing your full contact information.

Thanks for considering LDP and Ca$h Presents.

CHAPTER ONE

It was a beautiful eight-three degrees outside, and the sun was beaming its brightest. All that could be heard were the hoots, hollers and screams of men, women and children that were enjoying their time at the block party. The setup looked like a small carnival, Dub car show and zoo, all in one. Anything you could think of was present and at the disposal of everyone in attendance. Needless to say, this was the most fun the hood had seen in many years, and all of the residents were happy for it.

The gathered communities owed their thanks to Lyndell Combs, an ex-crackhead turned crack kingpin. You see, Lyndell made his money by having his soldiers push his poison in the African American ghettos. His product destroyed the lives of many families so he felt that it was only right that he gave back to the very communities he was tearing apart by providing a day of fun, food and beverages. Sure his day of festivities would do little to ease all of the pain that he'd caused, but the way he looked at it, it was better than him not giving back at all.

Everyone was so engrossed in the good time that they were having that they'd forgotten about a very real threat hanging over their heads like a black cloud. Lyndell was engaged in a drug turf war with Boss Dawg Outlaw Gang, one of the biggest Mexican gangs in Southern California. So far, BDOG had been on the losing end, but Lyndell still had a significant list of casualties on his end. The ongoing conflict was the reason that Lyndell had assigned a very skilled security team to watch over the block party. He had niggaz dressed in all black army fatigues positioned at every corner, as well as every rooftop of every apartment building and house, with M-4s. Although security like this was costly, Lyndell felt like you couldn't put a price tag on a peace of mind.

Everyone from the nobodies to the somebodies was in attendance of the block party that day. Teenage kids and little boys and girls were zipping back and forth across the lawns of neighboring houses laughing and playing, seemingly oblivious to what the adults had going on, which was quite all right with them. Niggaz were wearing their best clothes and jewelry while women were wearing next to nothing, showing plenty of tits and ass. The chicks stood beside the owners of all of the fly ass cars/and or motorcycles, smiling and rubbing on them as they shot their mack. The owners of the motorcycles were either polishing the chrome pipes of their bikes or racing them up and down the block, stunting and showing off.

"Soooooo, who you eyeballing out here?" Yada asked her best friend, LeAndra aka LeLe. Yada was definitely a sight for sore eyes. She had the most beautiful milk chocolate complexion, and slanted eyes that made her look very exotic. She was a busty chick with a big old ass, and a shape like a 1957 *Coca Cola* bottle. At the moment her hair was parted straight down the middle with an afro puff on either side. She was wearing gold door knockers, a gold necklace with her nickname, Yada, a baby T-shirt that displayed the diamond stud in her navel, tight red shorts and low top All Star Chuck Taylor Converses.

Yada was a street kid. Her first taste of the lifestyle came when she started setting niggaz up for her father to rob so they could keep clothes on their backs and a roof over their heads. Yada was very instrumental in the rise of her father's drug empire. She used to cook up the crack and transport the weight across state lines during the operations fundamental stage. But those days were far behind her now. These days she didn't touch drugs of any kind. Nah, she ran her own hair salon.

"Shit, nobody really, these niggaz got money but not the swagger to match." LeLe assured her bestie as she ate a big ass pickle. LeLe was a redbone chick with a hairstyle like Jada Pinkette Smith in the Jason's Lyric movie. She wore bamboo earrings, oversized designer shades, and a Rolex necklace. She also had gold rings on every finger and thumb. As of now, she was wearing a halter top underneath a yellow Bell-Air academy baseball jersey, white jean shorts and untied construction Timberland boots. Both, Yada and LeLe was twenty-two-years-old.

"That's all you care about? Money and swagger?"

"Yeah, and a big ol' dingaling."

Yada laughed and gave her a high-five, saying, "Girl, you too much."

"What about chu? You see anybody you like out here?" LeLe scanned their surroundings. Everyone was talking, joking, and laughing, having themselves a good old time. The men she did come across ranged from average looking to somewhat attractive.

"Please, even if I wanted to give one of these niggaz the time of day, they're not fucking with me." Yada claimed as she looked over her French tip, manicured nails.

"What?" LeLe popped the pickle from out of her mouth. "How you figga that?"

She stopped examining her manicure and turned to her, saying, "My daddy. These niggaz are petrified of Lyndell Combs."

"That's 'cause they know if they come at chu then they better have your best intentions at heart. Or they gon' end up with a cap in their ass. Uncle Lyndell don't play that shit behind his only daughter." she started back eating the pickle. "if you ask me, he's doing you a favor, weeding out all the dog ass niggaz that don't wanna do nothing but get up in dem draws. You feel me?" she turned to her smiling and dapping her up.

"I feel you. But even if he wasn't around, I know what a nigga be on when he tryna holla from jump. Daddy taught me well."

Suddenly, a saddened look came over LeLe's face, as she thought back to her father. You see, in the beginning of Lyndell's drug operation, he employed his best friend, Will Sax, and his girlfriend, Stella McLeod, to traffic kilos of cocaine for him across state lines. During this time, eleven-years-ago, there was a war between the BDOG, just like now. The couple was ambushed in the middle of the road by BDOG assassins with AK47s, who pumped their vehicle full of lead, Swiss cheesing it.

When her parents were murdered, Lyndell took LeLe into his home and raised her like she was his blood. This was the reason why Yada and LeLe were more like sisters than best friends.

A sorrowful look crossed Yada's face when she realized that her friend was hurting over the loss of her parents. She hugged her against her breasts and rubbed her back, comfortingly. She then kissed the top of her head.

"I'm sorry, boo, but it's gonna be all right. It's gonna be alllll right. I promise you." Yada held her eyelids shut as she continued to rub LeLe's back. She listened to her cry for a moment. Then, LeLe pulled back from her, wiping her dripping eyes and smiling.

"Look at my ol' cry baby ass. I'm too old for this shit."

"Pain never gets old, girl. The death of loved ones always stays with us. It just gets a little easier to deal with as each day goes by," Treasure wiped away her friend's tears with her thumbs, then kissed her on the forehead, and hugged her once more.

LeLe finished off her pickle and threw the wrapping into the trashcan, brushing her hands across each other. "Ok, now back to the subject of men."

"I was telling you how none of them were fucking with me on the account of my old man."

"Right," she pointed at her grinning. "But I know two dudes that'll gladly risk their lives to get next to you."

"Who?"

"Voss and that nigga, Jabar."

"Jabar," Yada frowned up, like saying his name disgusted her. "Girl, Jabar is not my type."

"Jabar's ugly ass isn't anyone's type, with his Craig Mack looking ass. I wouldn't fuck him with another bitch's pussy."

"Hahahahaha," Yada doubled over laughing with her hand over her stomach. "Yo, that's fucked up you said that. You ain't right."

"Maybe not, but I'm speaking facts." LeLe smiled happily.

"Ok. Now what about Voss, then."

"Voss," she nodded as she thought about him. "I like Voss. I think he's perfect for you."

"You think so?"

"I know so."

"I think he's cute, but I don't know girl. That nigga has wayyyy too many hoes for me."

"True. But if he didn't have any, you'd be wondering what the fuck was wrong with him. And you wouldn't wanna give 'em a shot. Now am I wrong or right?"

Yada thought it over for a second and nodded, saying, "Yes."

"See."

Vroooooooom!

A Harley Davidson Sports Glide whipped past Yada and LeLe ruffling their hair and clothing. The Harley swung around and slid to a stop before a cluster of six African American men wearing black leather vests with their motorcycle club's name on it. All of the men wore a purple scarf of some kind, either around their neck, wrist, or out of their right back pocket. Even their motorcycles had the color purple on them. The motorcycle's club name was The Venoms. Their logo had their clubs name at the top, California, which was their chapter at the bottom, and three purple snake heads in the center. The snake head in the middle was most noticeably bigger than all of the others.

The driver of the Harley Davidson Glide put down the kickstand and killed the engine of his bike. He then dismounted the hog, removing his gloves and stuffing them into his right back pocket. Afterwards, he took off his black, spiked helmet and hung it on the left handlebar of his motorcycle. When he did this it revealed his hairstyle which was locs. His scalp was greased and the locs were braided into four neat plats. When the driver looked back up, he locked eyes with LeLe through his black Aviator shades. He smiled and his bushy mustache stretched across his upper lip, setting off the gap between his teeth. LeLe smiled back at him, as she curled her hair around her finger. She couldn't get over how handsome and masculine homeboy was. He was tall too.

He stood six-foot-three, and had a muscular physique. She could tell he frequented the gym. The nigga was built like he should be wearing a cape and fighting crime. He had a thick ass neck and muscular arms, all of which were loaded with tattoos. The driver of the Harley was wearing a long sleeve purple T-shirt underneath his black leather vest, black denim jeans and Air Force Ones. His wallet chain hung low and was attached to his wallet which was inside of his right back pocket.

The driver of the Harley kept staring in LeLe's direction as his boys came over and greeted him, slapping him five. One of them popped the cap off a Heineken with his trusty bottle-opener and handed him the beer which he took a moment to chug down halfway. He chopped it up with his brothers for a minute before excusing himself and heading in LeLe and Yada's direction, taking the occasional swig of his Heineken as he advanced in their direction.

Excited, LeLe turned to Yada, "Girl, he's headed this way." LeLe proceeded to look in her best friend's shades, fixing her hair and adjusting her breasts in her top.

Yada glanced over LeLe's shoulder, seeing the driver of the Harley nearing them. "He sho is."

"Quick, how do I look?" she made a kissing face and turned her head from left to right.

"How you look? Like the same ugly ass bitch I've known more than half my life."

"Kiss my ass," as LeLe turned around from her, she smacked herself on the ass, causing Yada to bust up laughing. As soon as she was facing that nigga that was on that Harley, LeLe fronted as if he wasn't a big deal. You know, acting like she didn't even notice him and shit.

"Hello, how're you ladies doing? I'm Maul," the driver of the Harley extended his massive hand. LeLe and Yada introduced themselves as they shook his hand one at a time. While LeLe was smiling from ear to ear, Yada was plain faced.

"Pleasure to meet chu," Yada and LeLe said.

"Oh no, the pleasure is all mine," Maul smiled, showing off that gorgeous smile of his that was making LeLe moist between her legs. Still holding LeLe's hand, he bowed and planted a gentle kiss on it. She smiled and blushed, licking her lips and chuckling.

"Well, check you out, Mr. Smooth." LeLe said of his kissing her hand. "Sooooo, how long you been a member of The Venoms?"

"Forever and a day. I'm the president of my club."

"Oh, really? Sis," she glanced at Yada. "We've got ourselves a shot-caller here."

"I see." Yada smiled.

Tranay Adams

"What's that chu whipping over there, big daddy? A Harley?" LeLe looked around him.

He glanced over his shoulder and then turned back around, saying, "Yep."

"It's big. Real big," She openly admired the motorcycle.

"Well, uh, you know, I'm from Texas. So you know what they say…"

"Nah, what's that?" LeLe placed her nail at the corner of her teeth, looking at him seductively.

"Everything is big in Texas."

When he said this, LeLe was watching his mouth and for the first time she noticed that he had a mouth full of gold teeth, which gleamed when the sun kissed off of it. This shit turned her on. She loved dirty South niggaz that rocked los and gold grills. To her, there wasn't anything sexier than a thugged out ass nigga with tattoos and a Southern drawl.

"Is that so?" LeLe's eyes wandered down to his crotch. He had an impressive dick imprint.

"Facts." Homie smiled and took another drink of his Heineken, throat rolling up and down his neck.

"Well, I can't wait to find out…" LeLe began, tracing his huge pecks through his shirt. "Just how big…your pipe is…on your…motorcycle," LeLe looked up at him smiling hard, and taking his Heineken bottle. Staring him in the eyes, she slid her tongue up the neck of the bottle and slowly turned it up, drinking from it.

Yada rolled her eyes when she saw her girl do this shit. She then folded her arms across her breasts and took a deep breath, tapping her foot impatiently.

"Well, I could give you a personal tour of my motorcycle, and possibly take you for a ride. How'd you like that?"

"I'd love that," she passed him back his Heineken bottle and he took her hand, leading her towards his hog.

As she was pulled along, a smiling LeLe turned to Yada and waved goodbye. "I'ma get witchu later, girl, why don't you go and holler at Voss with his fine ass?"

Yada nodded and went to see what there was for her to get into. Making her way across the street where she saw a crap game going on inside of a yard, she found children zipping back and forth across her, playing.

***

Six men stood in a circle next to wrinkled piles of money, watching in anticipation as Voss shook the dice in his fist. The sound of the white cubes with the black dots on them rattled hard in his balled hand. His brows had formed a scowl as he chewed softly on his tongue determined to hit his point. It was hot as fuck outside so his face was lightly shiny from perspiration, as well as his shoulders and chest. His chest rose and fell as he took hefty breaths. He was nervous believe it or not. He was ten thousand dollars in the hole. Although he was a gambler, today didn't seem to be his lucky day on the dice.

Voss was a six-foot-two nigga with blue eyes and skin so light he could pass for white. Almost all of him was covered in tattoos. He had shoulder-length golden brown hair, which he had braided into eight cornrows. His muscular physique filled out a sleeveless jean jacket with a white fur collar which he wore over his bare chest. He had several gold chains around his neck that varied in size, some of them being chokers. He also wore matching jean shorts which sagged off his ass and high-top Nike Air Force Ones.

Voss was the product of a Scottish whore and a Haitian trick whose condom broke while they were fucking in the backseat of his car. When his mother gave birth to him, she left the hospital thirty-minutes later to turn tricks for her pimp, leaving Voss a ward of the state. Voss bounced from foster home to orphanage until he eventually grew tired and ran away. He took up refuge in the streets stealing, robbing and sleeping in vacant lots and staircases.

At the tender age of thirteen, Voss made his bones as a notorious jack boy and killa which eventually garnered the attention of the ranking members of the Eastside Rolling 30s Bloods (BSP) who recruited him. For a while he ran the streets wild and out of control, until Lyndell cleaned him up and brought him into his operation, utilizing his unique skills and talents. Since the kid had gotten down with Lyndell, the times of him eating out of trash cans and stuffing cardboard in his holey sneakers were gone. He lived the good life now, enjoying the finer things that money could buy.

"What chu down? What chu down?" Voss continued to rattle the dice in his fist as he pointed to the men in the circle asking them how much money they had betted. The men were either kneeling beside their pile of money or standing up beside it. They all called out what they were down, as soon as Voss pointed to them.

"I'm down a rack," Bang answered as he counted the fat stack of blue face one-hundred dollar bills in his hand. He was a skinny nigga that didn't stand a hair over five-foot-nine. He had tattoos, but his Burberry black complexion hid them. Right then he was wearing a camouflage Mariners baseball jersey over his bare chest with several unique gold chains and matching pants.

"Ok," Voss replied and then pointed to Jabar. "You?"

Jabar smacked his lips and looked up at Voss. "My nigga, money down!"

"How much though, my nigga?"

"You got big bank, you can fade it."

Voss looked away and blew his hot breath, frustrated. He then looked back at Jabar. "I didn't ask you all that, homie. How much you down?"

"This nigga scared of money, Bang," Jabar shook his head. He then used his foot to spread the dead presidents out beside him, revealing exactly how much money he had down on the concrete, three thousand dollars. "Three bands!"

"Damn, nigga, was that hard?" Voss shook his head angrily, and shook the dice real good in his hand. "Coming out!" he called out, announcing to the betting players. Voss threw the dice out and the danced across the concrete, one stopped on six while two kept on spinning. The second one stopped on six, leaving the third one slowly coming down from its spinning. Voss's hopes were high. He knew if he had another six he'd have three of a kind and win. Anything less would result in the betting men trying to beat his point. That's if the remaining dice didn't stop on *one*.

"Fuck, Blood!" Voss called out of frustration. He then went around the circle paying mothafuckaz off. Once he was done, he asked everyone what they were down. They told him and he picked the dice back up, shaking them bitchez in his fist. He was about to unleash them when a sexy young thang caught his eye, moving towards him in what appeared like slow motion. Voss had seen her every day, but her beauty never paled. In fact, it seemed as if she got more attractive as the days went by. He was willing to bet his life savings on it. Anyway, the sexy young thang making her way in his direction was the lovely, Yada.

"What's up, fellas?" Yada greeted the men at the crap game with a wave of her hand.

"Heyyyy, Yada!" the men greeted Yada with smiles on their faces, looking her up and down. Most of them looked like they wanted to rape her on the spot with their thirsty asses.

"That means you, too, Voss." Yada informed him while he was telling the men to throw down their bets.

"Couldn't be me, lil' mama, I gotta name. So if you talking to me, I suggest you use it," He capped.

Yada placed her hand on her hip and switched her weight to her foot, angling her head at him like Black chicks do when they can't believe you came at them a certain kind of way. "Well, excuuuuuse me, how're you doing, Voss?"

"I'm straight, tryna take these fools money out here." Voss put her in the know.

"Maybe you can if you shoot the goddamn dice, man!" Jabar told him, a look of frustration written on his face. Beads of sweat were on his forehead and the rest of him was shiny from perspiration. He wiped the beads from off his forehead with the back of his hand and started counting the money in his hands.

"That's all I'm saying." Bang said with a shiny face. He was fanning himself with a fat sack of hundreds and twenties, trying to keep cool. It was hot as a bitch out there!

Voss looked at them clown ass niggaz and waved them off; he didn't give a fuck about what they had to say. He was the bank and he'd shoot the dice whenever he got good and goddamn ready to.

"Well, uh, I'll leave you guys to it then," Yada moved to walk off, but Voss grabbed her hand, wanting her to stay.

"Nah, chill for a minute, you may change a nigga'z luck for the good." He told her.

"Ok. I ain't got shit to do anyway."

"Cool." Voss turned his attention back to the crap game and shook the dice in his fist, listening to them rattle. "Alright, y'all, I'm coming out the door! Foe, fifty, six!" he threw his hand forward and let the dice roll off of his palm. They danced across the ground spinning, shaking and moving like they'd done before. When they stopped, they stopped on four, five and six, which were winning numbers. The losing players looked salty as fuck as a smiling

Voss went around the circle picking up their money and stuffing the shit in his pockets. From then on, Voss was on a winning streak, tearing their asses up. He was hitting so much that he broke Yada off a taste of his winnings and she gave him a big kiss on the cheek, leaving a red lipstick imprint kiss behind. That shit really gassed Voss up. Once he'd gotten that kiss, he vowed to send every nigga out there home broke.

"Alright, y'all, I'm coming out!" Voss announced once all of the men had placed down their bets. He shook up the dice and threw his hand out. The dice flew out of his hand and danced across the ground, doing like they'd done before. Two of the dice stopped on five while the other fell inside of a crack, appearing to be either *five* or a *one*. If it was *five* then Voss was a winner but if it was *one*, then Voss was a loser. The dice showed *five* on Voss's side and *one* on Jabar's side. "That's what I'm talking about, baby! Don't nobody in this bitch move!" he called out, going around the circle picking up the money and stuffing it inside of his pockets. When he'd reached for Jabar's money, the nigga snatched it up.

"Nigga, you got me fucked up! That's an ace all day, dawg!" A scowling Jabar pointed to the ace with the hand he held most of his money in.

"My nigga, put the money back down on the ground before you find yo self in a situation." A scowling Voss warned Jabar. His arms were at his sides and his fists were clenched.

Jabar frowned up and narrowed his eyelids into slits, tilting his head to the side like *Nigga, what?* "You threatening me, dawg?"

"Not at all, I'm warning you." Voss, seeing that he was going to have a problem, stuffed all the money he'd gathered into all of his pockets.

"What's gon' happen if I don't put it down? Huh? What the fuck is gon' happen?" Jabar asked. Once he asked this, Bang stood up beside him.

"Nigga, I ain't finna play witcho bitch ass!" Voss snapped and pulled out his banga. Jabar had drawn his from his waistline at the same time. They both had their guns pointed at each other. The third gun to come into play was Bang's and it was pointed at Voss.

As soon as the bangaz were drawn the niggaz at the crap game scattered like roaches, abandoning their cups of alcohol and bottle of liquor. The only people left behind were the men and Yada, who was tucked safely behind Voss where he had put her.

"You ready to die, nigga?" Jabar spat at Voss.

"Right after you," Voss countered.

Voss and Jabar were about to pull the triggers of their weapons, when a deep, baritone voice rang out, halting their initial action.

"What the hell is going on here? Y'all pulling this shit in broad daylight with people's kids around?" Lyndell said as he came walking over from the BBQ grill, large fork in hand. He was wearing a baseball cap and an apron that read 'I heart cookin'. An angry expression was fixed on his face. He was in the middle of flipping over the meat on the grill when he saw the gangsta scene unfolding not too far from him.

Lyndell was a six-foot-three African American man, fifty-two years in age. He had a golden brown complexion, ashy looking skin, and black rings around his eyes. He rocked a head full of naturally, graying curls and a thick salt and pepper beard. He'd almost always dressed in something formal, and when he wasn't he'd be in a polo shirt and jeans. Lyndell looked nothing like the crack king that the streets know him as, and every bit of a university professor, especially when he'd wore his glasses.

Lyndell made his way through a crowd of small children and adults who were looking on in amazement wondering what was going to happen next. This angered Lyndell. Today was supposed to be a day of celebration and fun, and it looked like Voss and Jabar was about to fuck that up.

Lyndell snatched his baseball cap off his head, and smacked Voss and Jabar, saying, through gritted teeth, "Put 'em down! Put them goddamn guns down, now!" his head snapped from left to right, looking both gangstaz in the eyes.

"No can do, OG! Ain't nobody finna chump me for my grips!" Voss stated, scowling harder.

"Chump you how?" Lyndell frowned up, wondering just what the fuck Voss was getting at.

Jabar went on to inform Lyndell exactly what the disagreement was regarding the dice. When Lyndell looked down at the dice, and how they were positioned, he looked back up at Jabar. "You in the wrong all day, Jabar!"

"Fuck you figga that?" Jabar snapped.

"It's clear as day that that dice is showing a five. It's not forming a diamond pyramid."

Jabar lowered his gun to his side and so did Voss. "Man, Lyndell, why the fuck you always taking this nigga side, dawg? I mean, what the fuck does he have on you?"

Bang tucked his gun at the small of his back. He could already see that this beef wasn't going anywhere.

"Right is right and wrong is wrong, son. Had it been you that shot them dice then I'd be taking up for you."

Just then, Voss snatched up the pile of money he had bet with Jabar, stuffing it all in both of his pockets.

"Look," Lyndell began, smacking his baseball cap on his head and adjusting it to his liking. "I don't want any shit outta you two so I'ma gon' head and break you off that lil' bit of change ya lost. How much was ya loss?" he fished around inside of his pants pocket and pulled out a big ass wad of money, counting through it.

"Man, it ain't about the money, it's about the principal." Jabar stated, mad dogging Voss.

"Nothing to do with principal, it's more about pride. And believe you and me; I know what it's like to be a man with pride. You'll be willing to risk it all for what you feel is right."

"Even yo life." Voss shot back subliminally, hinting to Jabar he was going to die that day.

When Voss said that shit, Jabar gritted and a vein bulged at his temple as he clenched his fists.

"How much you hit 'em for, Voss?" Lyndell asked as he pulled a second big ass wad from his other pocket.

"About three grand, OG," Voss answered.

With that having been said, Jabar counted up three grand and gave it to Jabar. Jabar snatched the money out of Lyndell's hand while he continued to mad dog Voss, and stuffed it inside of his jeans pocket.

"Well, ain't chu gon' say thank you?" Lyndell said of the money he'd gifted him with.

"Fuck no!" Jabar said then looked over his shoulder at Bang. "Come on, dawg, let's bounce up outta here." Jabar brushed past Lyndell and made his way past Voss, looking him up and down with a snarl. He then continued out of the gate, making his way past children and their parents who were still watching the entire ordeal.

Right then, a nursery song filled the air as an ice cream truck neared. Seeing the children grow excited, Lyndell thought that now was a good time to get their minds off of what just happened and gave them all a few dollars to get whatever they wanted from off of the truck. The kids thanked him and ran off, some of them falling and getting back up, anxious to catch up with the ice cream truck before it had gone. Lyndell looked on smiling at them. He loved children and hoped Yada would bare him some grandchildren of his own.

Once the children were out of sight, Lyndell turned his attention on Yada and Voss who had just tucked his gun at the small of his back. "What the fuck is wrong with that boy?" he asked of that nigga Jabar.

"I don't know, G. But he's gon' fuck around and get his cap peeled messing with me. That'll be that niggaz last time pulling a strap out on me and not using it. Him and his mothafucking flunky, that's on Piru!"

Lyndell took a deep breath and said, "I understand where you're coming from, trust me. But let's hope that it doesn't go that far."

"You better talk to that nigga."

"I will. I'll give 'em a call once I figured he's cooled off."

"Good."

"You all right?" Lyndell focused his attention on his daughter, Yada.

Yada approached her father, and he threw his arm around her shoulders. She then kissed him on his cheek which caused him to chuckle and smile. "Yeah, I'm fine."

"Good." He kissed her on the head. "'Cause let something had happened to you on the account of these two knuckleheads, and I wouldn't have spared any expense to have them and everyone apart of their bloodline erased from off the face of this earth." Yada kissed him on the cheek again. Lyndell made sure he gave Voss the evil eye when he said what he'd said. Now, don't get it fucked up. He loved Voss like he'd skeeted him out of his dick-head, but he loved his precious daughter that much more. She meant everything to him, and he'd be damned if he lost her on account of some bullshit and niggaz not pay the price for it.

"Daddy, if it means anything to you, before things got too hectic, Voss pulled me to the back of him so I wouldn't be hurt."

"Of course he did, sweetheart. I love this young nigga like a son. But he knows what I'd do to anyone that has something to do with my baby girl getting hurt or killed, no matter what they mean to me. Ain't that right, baby boy?"

"Yeah, I know. Just like you know that any mothafucka you send at me, I'd be sending 'em back with their heads knocked off, ain't that right, OG?"

Voss and Lyndell stared one another down, intensely. Yada looked back and forth between them both, looking worried, hoping they weren't about to start fighting. Suddenly, a smile spread across Lyndell's face and he started laughing low at first, and then loudly. A smile spread across Voss's face too. And then one came across Yada, seeing that the men were just fucking with one another and weren't serious.

"That's what I'm talking about. My young nigga ain't scared of nobody, not even me. You're a gangsta about yours," Lyndell hugged Voss. He then hugged him and patted him on his back, kissing him on the temple.

"You had me a lil' worried there, G. I was starting to think you weren't playing with a nigga." Voss told him.

"Shiiiit, I couldn't tell. You looked like you were ready to pop off." He chuckled as they broke their embrace.

"Hell, I was. Like you said 'I'ma gangsta about mine.'"

"My nigga," Lyndell said like Denzel in *Training Day*, hugging him again. "The meat should be done by now. Y'all hungry?" he slipped his arms over Voss and his daughter's shoulders, walking back towards the BBQ grill.

"I could eat," Yada replied.

"Man, I'm starving like Marvin."

"Good. 'Cause we've got plenty to eat."

CHAPTER TWO

After Voss and Yada had eaten, they chilled out front, chopping it up and taking swigs of ice cold Coronas. They reminisced about old times and current events, laughing their asses off. Yada found herself growing increasingly touchy feely towards Voss, and so did he. Without even realizing it they were walking around holding hands. Their connection seemed to have come naturally since they'd had crushes on one another since they were kids, but had never pursued anything. Neither one of them was tripping though because the way they saw it, it was better for things to blossom now rather than later.

Having found it growing cold outside, Voss slipped his jean jacket off and over Yada's shoulders. Still holding hands, he and Yada continued up the block chopping it up, taking in their surroundings.

"Looks like everyone is starting to leave," Yada said to Voss as she looked at some of the attendants of the block party gather their friends and family to head home.

"Yeah," Voss agreed, making the same observation.

"I'm definitely not ready to take it in."

"Me either," he pulled out his cellular and looked at the time on the display. It was almost seven o'clock. He stuck the cell phone back inside of his pocket and said, "Look, since neither of us is ready to go home, how 'bout we go golfing? I know a place that stays open pretty late."

"Hey, I'm with that."

"It's a date then?" He looked at her with a smile. He'd tried several times to get her to go out with him, but she'd always curved him. Before he stepped out with her tonight he wanted confirmation that they were going on a real date.

"Yep. It's a date." She smiled.

Vrooom! Vrooom! Vrooom!

The Venoms blew past Voss and Yada on their motorcycles, stealing their attention. When they looked up, they found Maul bringing up the rear of his club, with LeLe sitting on the back of his Harley with her arms wrapped around his waist. LeLe was smiling like hell. She found the experience of riding on homeboy's motorcycle exciting. She was wearing Maul's helmet while his head went unprotected.

"Heyyyy, boo, I see you got cho man!" LeLe called out over the loud engine of the Harley. Her observation caused Yada to turn red with embarrassment, and Voss glanced at her, grinning. Now he knew for sure that Yada was feeling his ass.

"Anywayyy, where yo ass off to?" Yada inquired.

"Girl, we're going to Roscoe's Chicken & Waffles, y'all tryna roll?"

"Yeah, y'all are welcome to come. It's my treat." Maul said, looking from Voss to Yada for their reply.

"We'll have to take a rain check; we've got something else going."

"Oooooh, ok," LeLe smiled harder, looking between Voss and Yada. "Well, Voss, you make sure you bag it before you tag it."

With that having been said, Maul sped off on the Harley before Yada could reply. LeLe threw her head back and gave a throaty laugh.

"That girl is something else," Yada shook her head, smiling. "Come on, handsome, let's tell my dad we're leaving." Yada led Voss into the direction where her father was talking to a couple of his henchmen.

"So, what made you agree to go out with me this time, as oppose to all of the others?" Voss asked Yada as he practiced his swing. He'd cock his club back and bring it dangerously close to the golf ball, several times, trying to make sure he'd get the ball as close to the hole as he could.

"I don't know," Yada smiled and shrugged. "I guess the vibe. I mean, I always found you attractive, and I would have went out with chu before, but to be frankly honest, nigga, you got wayyyy too many hoes. Shit, a bitch not tryna be just another name on the hit list."

Voss chuckled and said, "I feel you. But if you and I got together it wouldn't even be that kind of party. You aren't anything like them sack chasers I be fucking with. You're special...real special, so I gotta treat you as such."

Yada was smiling harder now. "You better."

"Soooooo, you said you didn't go out with me before 'cause I had too many hoes. Now what makes you think that I don't still have 'em?"

"Oh, I'm sure you do. But it's like you said, I'm special'. So, if this thing of ours goes any further, you're gonna have to drop them. That's part of you showing me that I am as special as you claim I am."

"That's right." Voss dapped her up. He then focused his attention back on his golf ball, cocking the club high above his head. He held the club there for a moment, and then he swung it with all of his might. The club whizzed though the air and struck the golf club, knocking it high as fuck in the air. Voss and Yada stood side by side, holding their hand above their brows, watching the ball soar across the sky. They watched as the ball dropped out of the sky, rolling fairly close to the hole he had in mind. "Come on." He nudged Yada and slung the club over his shoulder, walking over to the golf cart. He climbed into the small vehicle, behind the wheel and cranked it up. Once Yada was perched on the passenger seat, Voss drove off in the direction of the hole.

"Can I ask you something?"

"Nah, I'm tired of talking to yo ass!" A grinning Voss glanced at Yada. She was looking like *Nigga, what the fuck is your problem?* Which made him laugh. "I'm fucking witchu."

"Fat head!" she playfully punched him in his arm.

"Ow, that shit hurt!" he rubbed his arm.

"That's what chu get." She faked like she was angry. "Now, can I ask you a question or are you gonna be a smart ass about it?"

"Go ahead, shoot!"

"Do you ever see yourself being more than what chu are? I mean, do you ever see yo self not working with my father, and doing your own thing?" she looked at him in anticipation of what his answer would be.

"Hell yeah," he frowned up. "Look, I ain't like the rest of these niggaz working under yo pops, cool with eating off his plate 'til whenever. I wanna be my own man, and run my own shit. I'ma fuck with the heroin game. You know you can make a lot more money off of dog food than crack. I just gotta save up enough dough to make one big buy, then I'ma be straight. Besides, fucking with the dope, I won't be stepping on yo pops' toes. You feel me?"

"Yeah, I feel you." She replied. "How much money do you have stashed now?"

"Shit, like, $300,000 dollars. I figure once I hit a meal ticket I'll be ready to go shopping. Already gotta plug that's gon' gimme a sweet deal."

"Well, check lil' daddy out. Baby out here making moves," Yada smiled at him and applauded.

"You damn right. Slow feet don't eat. Here we go," Voss pulled the golf cart over. He and Yada grabbed their golf clubs and jumped out; approaching the hole he had in mind. "You up for a lil' wager, beautiful?"

"Sure am, handsome, what do you have in mind?" Yada smiled excitedly.

"If I make this shot you gimme a kiss on the cheek, and if I miss, I give you a stack." He pulled a fat ass wad of dead faces from out of his pocket, counted out ten one-hundred dollar bills and stuck them into his opposite so they'd be visible. "We gotta deal?" he extended his and to her, smiling.

Yada looked from his hand to the shot; it looked impossible for him to make. So she went ahead and shook his hand, saying, "Deal."

"Hold my jacket for me, love." Voss removed his jacket and passed it to Yada. He then practiced swinging his club at the golf ball, bringing his club dangerously close to the ball with each swing. With a British accent, he said, "My lady, get ready to pucker up."

Yada puckered up her lips and moved her head from left to right, tauntingly. It was her way of telling Voss that he was never going to kiss her because he was going to miss the shot.

Voss chuckled and focused his attention back on the golf ball. An expression of determination spread across his face, as he continued to practice swinging at the ball. The last time he brought the club around from a swing, it tapped the ball gently, sending it rolling forward. At first it looked like the ball was going to miss the hole, but it eventually sunk into the black hole.

When the golf ball fell to the hole, Voss turned around to Yada smiling hard as fuck. She was smiling too.

"I must admit, this is one bet I don't mind losing." She said.

"Well, is that right?"

"Yep. Now get cho fine ass over here," Yada pulled him closer to her by the front of his shirt. He gave her his cheek to kiss, but she turned his face around, kissing him on the mouth. She then slipped him a little tongue. They hummed and turned their heads counter clockwise away from one another. Their making out was intense and romantic.

***

Two vans rolled up to the shutter of an old factory, their headlights shining brightly. The van at the shutter honked its horn and a moment later the shutter was hastily rising, as someone on the inside was pulling on its chain. Once the shutter was up, the vans drove in over the threshold. The shutter was let down by one of Lyndell's goons who happened to be dressed in all black and wearing a black bandana over the lower half of his face. He slipped the strap of his M-16 over his shoulder and made his way over in the direction of the vans. Just then, the back doors of the rear van opened, and Jabar hopped out, dressed just like the nigga that had just opened the shutter. He helped Bang lumber a hostage out of the van, who was wearing a black pillowcase over his head. Jabar grabbed the hostage under his other arm, and together, he and Bang dragged his ass over to the center of the warehouse.

Jabar and Bang placed the hostage on his knees below two dangling ropes. Jabar held the hostage at gunpoint while Bang chopped off the duct tape that bound his wrists. Once Bang relieved the hostage of his restraints, he sheathed his knife and began tying the ropes around his wrists tightly. Afterwards, Bang grabbed the opposite end of the two conjoining ropes and nodded to Jabar. Jabar tucked his gun on his waistline and snatched the black pillowcase off of the hostage's head. As soon as he did this, the hostage looked up at him with a bloody, battered face. The hostage had a huge knot on the side of his forehead. One of his eyes was swollen shut, and his lips had ballooned. They were busted.

Bloody slime and snot oozed out of his nose and dangled off his chin. The collar of his undershirt was stained pink from his bleeding. The hostage's head bobbled when he brought it up to look up at Jabar who was standing over him. With overwhelming hate, Jabar suddenly kicked him in his temple. The hostage slumped on the ropes and bowed his head, moaning in agony.

"Pussy ass mothafucka! That was some ho ass shit chu did back there, and if it was up to me, I'd chop off yo dick and balls." With that having been said, Jabar turned around to the van behind him and motioned for someone to get out. A second later the passenger door opened and Lyndell hopped out, casually strolling over in the hostage's direction. Lyndell's face was frowned up as he approached the hostage. He was wearing the same clothing that he was wearing at the block party except he wore a jacket over it. There were speckles of dried blood on his neck and hands he'd neglected to rinse all of the way off. When the shooting first happened, Lyndell made sure that the victim was hauled off to the hospital as soon as possible, then he ran back to one of the houses and used the water hose to wash the blood from off him. That's when he got a hit through his ear-bud that Jabar and Bang had apprehended the culprit in question.

"Out of all the killaz Valdez could send at me, he sent chu. A goddamn novice who can't even shoot straight. You know that lil' girl you shot tryna kill me was only six-years-old? Her birthday was two days ago," Lyndell's eyes had grown glassy. He found his voice cracking under his emotions so he bowed his head and cleared his throat, trying his best to gather himself before he continued on with what he had to say. Once he did he looked back up at the BDOG assassin, mad dogging him, vein pulsating at his temple, with his jaws clenched. He saw through a haze of red, looking through his eyes. "Two days ago, cocksucka!"

Bwap! Wop! Bap!

Lyndell gave the BDOG a three punch combination, whipping his head in every direction. When his head came back down, he lifted it back up and spat slimy globs of blood on the floor. Lyndell looked down at the nasty goo in disgust. He then pulled out a pair of black leather gloves from his back pocket, pulling them over his hands and wiggling his fingers inside of them. He then turned his attention to Bang, motioning him over and saying, "Lemme borrow that knife of yours youngin'."

Snikt!

Bang drew his knife from where he had it sheathed. A gleam swept up the length of the blade. Once Bang finally reached Lyndell, he handed him the deadly blade by its handle and took a step back.

"You're gonna pay dearly for what chu done, homeboy. I'm gonna take my pint of flesh now," Lyndell grabbed him by the face and turned it to the side, displaying the tattoo on the assassin's neck. It was BDOG and the George Town Hoyas mascot dog's face. Holding the killa's face still, Lyndell began carving the tattoo up from his flesh, causing blood to run in a small river.

"Aaahhhhh! Ahhhhh!" the BDOG assassin's eye bulged and he hollered aloud, displaying his bloody mouth and missing teeth. He struggled on the ropes his wrists were bound to, but they wouldn't give; they held him firmly.

"I bet chu regret your decision now, huh? Don't chu, you fucking scumbag," Lyndell gritted his teeth, bringing his knife around to continue the carving out of the flap of flesh.

The BDOG assassin, Lennox, had gotten dressed up like one of the security team members at the block party with a sniper rifle. He holed up on one of the apartment building's rooftops and took aim at Lyndell. When the assassin pulled the trigger to deliver the kill-shot, most of the party goers had gone, so he believed he had a clean shot at Lyndell. But his execution was just a tad bit too late.

Lyndell was in the middle of sweeping the ground when he heard a little girl call after him. He looked up the block to see little Armiya, her eyes were big and her mouth was wide open, displaying her top row of missing teeth. In her hand was a thank you card that she'd made personally for him. It was to thank him for throwing the block party where she claimed she had 'the best day ever'.

"Mr. Combs, Mr. Combs!" Armiya ran at him full speed ahead. A smile stretched across Lyndell's face. He swept up the small pile of trash into the dust pan and dumped it inside of a nearby trash can. Afterwards, he sat the broom and dust pan aside. When he turned back around, Armiya was leaping up into the air. He caught her in his arms and hoisted her up. Glancing over his shoulders he saw her parents approaching wearing smiles on their faces just as big as their daughter's.

"Heyyyy, Armiya, what chu got there?" Lyndell asked the jolly child.

"It's a thank you card I made for you. I want chu to have it."

"Awww, you shouldn't have, limme see it."

Armiya went to hand him the card but she accidently dropped it. It floated to the ground, landing beside Lyndell's foot.

"Ooops, I'm sorry, Mr. Combs."

"It's ok, baby girl, I'll get it."

Holding Armiya in one arm, Lyndell bent down to pick up the thank you card and heard something whiz through the air. He then heard a gasp escape the child's lips. His eyes widened and he hoped he heard wrong, but unfortunately for him he didn't. When he looked to Armiya she had a red dot expanding at her chest, absorbing her dress. Her eyes were rolled to their whites and her mouth was hanging open.

"Oh, my God, no!" Armiya's mother called out.

"My baby!" her father called out.

Pulling out his gun from the small of his back, Lyndell looked around for where the shot had come from. He spotted the sniper on the rooftop of the apartment building. He looked like he was about to fire again, so Lyndell dove to the ground, pressing a dead Armiya to his chest. Still cradling the child to him, he crawled over to a parked car and took cover. He then contacted Jabar through his ear-bud, telling him to get Bang and go after the sniper on the apartment building's rooftop. He gave them a description of the complex as well as the address. It wasn't long before Jabar and Bang had captured dude.

Lyndell carried a lifeless Armiya over to her parents, handing her off to her father. He then ran across the street where he was told Jabar and Bang were holding the sniper hostage. Once he got to the garage of the complex, he and his goons beat the living shit out of the BDOG assassin. Lyndell called for his other goons to drive over in their vans. They duct taped the assassin's wrists and threw a black pillowcase over his head, throwing him into the back of one of the van's. Once Lyndell washed himself up with one of the water hoses and threw on his jacket, he climbed into one of the vans and they drove over to The House of Pain.

Once Lyndell had finished carving out the flap of flesh that boasted Lennox's BDOG tattoo, he tossed the bloody piece of skin to the floor. He then grabbed the top of the assassin's head and started slicing off his ears. The man screamed bloody murder, displaying every tooth and cavity inside of his grill. Lyndell then wrapped his hand around the lower half of his face and sliced off his nose like it was a piece of turkey. The severed nose fell off and deflected off the tip of Lyndell's shoe.

"Aahhhhh! Ahhhhh!" Lennox screamed and screamed with blood pouring from every hole in his face, dripping on the floor.

Lyndell looked at the bloody knife and then wiped it off on Lennox's shirt, handing it back to Bang who sheathed it on his hip. Lyndell then fished through his victim's pants pockets until he found his cellular. He scrolled through the contacts until he found the name he was looking for, Valdez. Having found the name, he called out to Jabar and Bang to grab the gas cans, which they did.

"Oh, please, God, no! Don't do this, don't do this to me! I'm begging you!" Lennox begged. There was a look of terror in his eyes. "You can just shoot me, you can just shoot meeee!" he made an ugly ass face and cried as he pleaded for his life. His entire body trembled and his teeth chattered uncontrollably.

"Shut cho faggot ass up!" Bang hauled off and punched Lennox square in the face, launching his head backwards and sending blood flying in every direction. The assault shut Lennox's ass up somewhat, but he was still whimpering like a fucking puppy.

While the poor bastard went on whimpering, Jabar and Bang splashed his sorry ass with gasoline until he was dripping wet with the shit. They then stepped back and Bang pulled out a Zippo lighter, producing a blue flame with a yellow tip. He looked over to Jabar who pulled the rope that bound Lennox's wrists, hoisting him higher and higher into the air. Bang then looked at Lyndell who had pulled out a Cuban cigar and dialed Valdez up on facetime. Lyndell smiled wickedly when he saw his enemy on the display.

"Lyndell, if it's your ugly face I'm seeing then I guess my boy, Lennox, missed his mark," Valdez said nonchalantly. He was young Mexican cat with a bald, tattooed head and a diamond stud nose piercing.

"Yeah. You guessed it," he went on to tell him that Lennox had accidently killed a little girl. This seemed to have saddened Valdez. He told Lyndell that he didn't mean for the little girl to get killed and that he only wanted him dead. "I figured you were a young man with old school principals. But still, an innocent child lost her life, so your sympathy changes nothing." Lyndell looked to Bang and he tossed the Zippo lighter up at Lennox. The flame of the lighter mingled with the flammable liquid and ignited Lennox. He danced as the fire swept over his entire body, engulfing him completely in flames.

"Aaaahhhhh! Aaahhhhhh! Aaaahhh!" Lennox screamed over and over again, tongue quaking inside of his mouth. He danced at the ends of the ropes as the fire ate away at his body, singing off his hair, eyebrows and mustache, and disintegrating his flesh.

Lyndell held up the cell phone so that Valdez could see his hitman burning to death. While he was doing this, he held up his cigar to the fire that was burning Lennox alive, lighting it. He took a couple of drags off of the cigar and blew out a big cloud of smoke.

"Next time...send your best when you coming at a gangsta, nigga!" Lyndell shouted out over Lennox's horrible screams. He allowed Valdez to watch the fire devour his hitta and eventually the ropes. The flames ate away the ropes that bound Lennox's wrists and his lifeless form fell from where it was suspended, crashing hard to the floor, his burning skull tumbling forward.

Lyndell turned the cellular so it would be facing him. He saw a very angry Valdez. "Next time I will not miss, mayate."

"For your sake, you better hope not." Lyndell stuck his cigar inside of his mouth, held up the middle finger to Valdez and then disconnected the call. He dropped the cell phone on the ground beside his foot, and stomped on it until it broke into pieces.

***

Voss pulled up in the driveway and he and Yada hopped out of the car. They were walking towards the house when a motorcycle pulled up, its headlight blinding them temporarily. They squinted their eyes and held a hand above their brows, trying to make out who it was on the bike. They stopped where they were and peered closer, seeing that it was Maul and LeLe. LeLe climbed off the back of the hog and passed Maul his helmet back, kissing him. As she walked away he smacked her on the ass so hard that the sound echoed throughout the night. LeLe didn't even wince as she adjusted her purse on her shoulder and walked towards the house like she had a broom stick up her ass.

Maul admired LeLe big old ass for a moment longer before he revved up his Harley and sped off, joining the rest of the Los Angelinos in city traffic.

"And just where are you coming from ho? I know it ain't Roscoe's with the way yo ass walking." Yada said as she unlocked the door and let everyone inside of the house, locking the door behind them.

LeLe looked at her and smiled. "We did go to Roscoe's, and afterwards we went back to Maul's house, and he beat this tiny lil' coochie up. Hadda bitch crawling the walls like Spider Man and shit, sis." She made noises like she was shooting webs, just like Spider Man.

Yada placed her hands over a chuckling Voss's ears and looked at LeLe like she was crazy, a slight grin on her face. "Bitch, shut cho mothafucking mouth, my man don't need to be hearing about cho thot adventures."

Knock, knock, knock, knock!

Yada's face balled up wondering who it could be rapping at her door. She approached the door and glanced through the peephole, relaxing once she saw who it was. She unchained and unlocked the door, pulling it open and stepping aside. When she did, her father, Lyndell, strolled inside of the house wearing a grim expression on his face. Once Yada shut and locked the door behind him, she approached him, hands on her hips.

"What's up, daddy? You look like something is wrong." Yada said with concern etched across her face.

Lyndell walked over to the couch and plopped down upon it, removing his apple jack hat from off his head. He flipped the hat over in his hands over and over again, looking like he was thinking about something. Once he was ready to finally speak, he looked around the room at everyone present.

"I guess y'all haven't heard yet. But after you guys left the block party tonight, lil' Armiya was shot and killed."

"Oh, my God, no!" Yada became teary eyed and placed her hands over the lower half of her face, sitting down next to her father. He lifted his arm and curled it around her, comfortingly.

"Yeah, they killed her while I was holding her in my arms, too. Blew a hole in that poor baby's chest," Lyndell shook his head shamefully. He was filled with great grief, believing that Armiya's death was his fault. He knew that if he hadn't thrown that party that the child would still be alive, and no one else could tell him any different. He'd have to live with the child's blood on his hands for as long as he lived.

"Oh, daddy, I'm so sorry." Yada kissed him on the cheek and wrapped her arms around his neck. He rubbed her arm soothingly and pecked her on the cheek. A saddened LeLe then sat on the couch beside Lyndell and laid her head in his lap. He rubbed her arm affectionately, giving her the same attention that he gave his daughter. He loved both of these women like they'd came from out of him.

"You ok, OG?" Voss asked from the arm of the reclining chair, folding his arms across his chest. A serious expression was fixed on his face.

"Yeah," Lyndell nodded. "I relieved a lil' stress before I came over here."

"Oh, yeah?"

"Yeah," he gave him a look that let him know that he'd killed the shooter.

"I got chu."

"Look," Lyndell started up again, addressing everyone present. "I know y'all kids aren't gon' stay locked up in the house no matter how much I stress that it ain't safe out there in them streets. So what I do want you to do is, be careful. Be very, very careful. These people that we're waging this war with are dangerous. In fact, they're probably the most dangerous that I've ever dealt with."

Yada pulled her face away from her father and wiped her eyes with the backs and palms of her hands, sniffling. "Ok, daddy, I'll be careful."

After she said this, Lyndell looked down at LeLe for her to agree that she'd be careful.

"You got it, Uncle Lyndell, I'll be careful."

"Good, it will help me sleep better. And you," he looked up at Voss.

"I'm already knowing, OG. I'll grow eyes at the back of my head, and as far as the ladies, I promise you won't nothing happen to them that doesn't happen to me first."

"Now that's what I like to hear." Lyndell kissed Yada and LeLe on the side of their head.

CHAPTER THREE
A couple of nights later

Voss and Yada had spent the night eating ice cream at Baskin' & Robin's and skating at World on Wheels skating ring. Voss couldn't skate for shit, so Yada spent most of her time helping him up on his feet, and convincing him to give skating another try. Having grown frustrated with trying, Voss gave up and decided to play the sidelines, watching his girl skate around the ring. Once they'd grown tired of skating they played games at the arcade, and shot across town to a hole in the wall spot on the lower Eastside called The Bar Fly where they threw back a couple of cold ones and shot a few games of pool. Now here they were back at Yada's place.

"Hahahahahahahahaha!" Yada threw her head back laughing heartily, placing her hand on Voss's shoulder. "Bae, you are lying. I know that did not really happen."

"I swear to God." Voss responded. "You wanna knowa lil' secret?"

"Sure."

"Any time I lie, my right eyelid will twitch."

"Hmmm. That's interesting."

"Go ahead. Ask me a question, so I can lie and you can see for yo self."

"Aren't you handsome?"

"Nah, ma, I'm ugly as fuck."

Yada looked closely at Voss's right eyelids, and sure enough, it twitched.

"Wow," Yada smiled. "That shit is really real."

"Yep." He smiled back at her.

There was silence between the two youngsters, as they were wrapped up in their thoughts. Yada would be the first to break that silence when she spoke up.

"Soooooo, would you like to come in for a nightcap?" A smiling Yada looked at Voss, hoping he'd say yes, interlocking her fingers with his fingers. They just jumped out of his car and were headed to Yada's house.

"I'm down. Long as you sure we aren't gonna run into yo homegirl again," Voss smiled back at her.

She chuckled and said, "I'm pretty sure we won't be running into LeLe. She has a date tonight so she won't be home."

"Alright then, nightcap it is." They kissed twice.

"I know Le ass didn't leave the front door open when she left." Yada frowned up as she looked at the front door, which was cracked open.

"Hmmm, I wonder. Come on, let's check it out." Voss crept up the front steps of Yada and LeLe's house, bringing her along the way. Once he got to the front door, he peeked inside. His eyes bulged and his mouth hung open. He couldn't believe his eyes but he was sure they weren't lying to him. LeLe was in her bra and panties, with a gag around her neck, tied to a chair. Her eyeliner had run from her crying her eyes out, as snot threatened to drip from her nose. A nigga dressed in all black wearing a ski mask over his face, stood before her, gun pointed at her kneecap.

"Pinche mayate whore, if ju don't tell me where Kenyatta Combs is I'll blow jour fucking kneecap off!" the masked up nigga threatened.

Voss and Yada exchanged shocked expressions when they heard the masked man asking about her whereabouts.

"I don't know! I don't know where she is! I swear to God! All I know is she gone out on a date!"

"Ju fucking lie!" he smacked her across the face with the butt of his gun, splitting her right cheek bloody and bruising it. She broke down sobbing with globs of slimy green snot hanging out of her nose.

"Noooo! I'm not! I don't know where she is you've gotta believe me…" she trailed off, bowing her head, breaking down sobbing again. Big teardrops fell from her eyes, hitting her knees and bare feet.

"Bullshit!" the masked man pulled her head back by her hair causing her to shriek. "Ju take me for a horse's ass! I know ju know something cause ju live together. So, I'm going to give ju 'til the count of three to tell me where she is and if ju don't tell me, then I'm going to blow jour brains out!"

"No, no, no, please, don't…" LeLe sobbed and trembled all over. The way she was shaking you would have thought she was sitting butt naked inside of a freezer.

Voss's face balled up with hatred watching what was going on. He hated niggaz that put they hands on females. To him, any nigga that dared to put his hands on the opposite sex was straight pussy, no exceptions.

"Oh, my God, he's gonna kill her. We've gotta do something, babe," Yada said in a whisper, peering into the house over Voss's shoulder.

"I know," Voss went to grab his gun from off his waistline, and grabbed air. His forehead creased, and he lifted up his shirt, looking down at his naked waist. That's when he remembered that he'd accidently forgotten his gun in the car. "Fuck!" he said angrily, balling up his fist.

"What? What's wrong?" Yada's face wrinkled with worry.

"I forgot my strap in the car."

"Damn."

"Fuck it. It's do or die!" Voss said as he rolled up the sleeves of his shirt, preparing himself for hand to hand combat.

"Voss, wait, I can go get it!"

"No time!" Voss pushed open the front door gently, making his way inside of the house as quietly as he could.

The masked up nigga, who was obviously Mexican, stepped back from LeLe and pointed his gun at her dome piece, counting down, "Won...

LeLe squeezed her eyelids shut and bowed her head, tears and snot dripping from off her chin. She continued to tremble, as he recited a prayer, "Have mercy on me, God, have mercy! I look to you for protection. I will hide beneath the shadow of your wings until the danger passes by."

"Two," the masked up nigga continued. "Thr—"

Splocka!

Voss appeared out of nowhere and kicked the gun up toward the ceiling. He then kicked the masked up nigga in the chest, slamming him up against the wall. Voss rushed him throwing a flurry of punches into his midsection. He then punched the masked man across the face twice. He was just about to uppercut the masked up dude, when he swung on him. Voss grabbed his arm and flipped him over his shoulder. Right after he wrapped his arms and leg around the masked up nigga's arm, locking it into place. Staring down at him through hatred plagued eyes, Voss broke his arm in half. Following up, he snapped the mothafucka's neck with the violent twist of his ankles. Once the masked up dude was staring up at the ceiling with vacant eyes, Voss released his arm, letting it fall to the floor lifelessly.

"Come on!" Voss motioned for Yada to come inside of the house. She rushed inside. Together, they untied the ropes that bound LeLe to the chair. Then, Voss pulled the gag from out of her mouth.

"There's another one inside of the house!" LeLe screamed out the warning.

At that moment Voss looked up at the mirror hanging on the wall, seeing another masked up nigga with a gun pointed at Yada. Acting off instinct, Voss tackled the girls out of the way just as the masked man fired his gun. *Splocka!* The bullet seemed to have been traveling in slow motion, and so did Voss and he fell toward the carpeted floor. Voss had almost cleared the path of the bullet when it entered his arm, exploding the fabric of his shirt, sending blood flying everywhere. Voss's eyelids squeezed shut as he threw his head back, screaming aloud.

Voss and the girls hit the floor with a thud. He bawled in pain, holding his arm, blood seeping between his fingers. He appeared to be in agony. Yada and LeLe rushed over to him trying desperately to help him up. They saw the second masked up nigga heading in their direction, to finish them off.

"Run, run, get out of here!" Voss called out to the girls. Yada was trying to stay to help him, but LeLe was pulling her along. LeLe was looking back and forth between Voss and the masked gunman, knowing it was a matter of seconds before he was on top of them with his gun.

Finally, Yada allowed LeLe to pull her away. They took off running toward the kitchen. Yada had disappeared inside another bedroom while LeLe was busy unlocking the backdoor. The masked gunman had just run into the living room, from the master bedroom, gun in hand. He looked in a terrified LeLe's direction, pointing his banga, pulling the trigger.

Splocka! Splocka!

A bullet entered the microwave and sparks flew. The other bullet hit the wall of the door frame, sending splinters flying. LeLe threw open the backdoor, jumping down into the grass and taking off running for her life.

The masked gunman looked down upon Voss angrily. He hated the fact that it was because of him that he missed the shot that he took at Yada. Voss mad dogged him, clenching his jaws so tight that a vein pulsated at his temple.

Keeping his eyes on the masked up gunman, Voss spat on the floor and said, "Handle yo business, mothafucka! I done seen everything but God anyway!"

"Adios," the masked up gunman pointed his banga down at Voss's face. He went to pull the trigger, and Yada appeared from his right, kicking the gun out of his hand. The gun flew across the room and deflected off the wall, splashing inside of the aquarium. Bubbles floated to the tank water's surface, as the gun sunk to the bottom, fish hurriedly swimming out of the way.

Yada moved with furious anger, giving him a three punch combo across the face. She then followed up by kicking him in the chest. The force from the kick sent the masked up nigga flying across the room, flailing his arms and legs. He crashed high up into the wall, knocking the plaster out of the wall. He fell to the carpeted floor hard. The mirror fixed on the wall fell and crashed on top of his head, shattering. The breakage left what looked like one-thousand glass shards scattered over the floor.

Yada stood where she was in a martial arts fighting stance, waiting for the masked up gunman to get up, breathing heavy. Once it looked like he was down for the count, she walked over to Voss, pulling him to his feet by his un-injured arm. Voss winced as he was helped upon his feet.

"You ok, babe?" Yada asked concerned. She went to take a look at his arm.

"Aaaahhhhhhh!" a roar of rage came from behind them. They looked over their shoulders to see the masked up nigga that Yada had taken out running at them. His ski mask and shoulders twinkled from the glass particles sprinkled over them. He was holding his gloved hands up, clutching large jagged shards of glass like they were knives. The tips of the shards twinkled beneath the lighting in the living room.

Bwop!

A 2 x 4 swung downward and exploded on impact against the back of the masked up gunman's head, dropping him to the carpeted floor. He lay there still, but breathing. Standing over him, still clutching what was left of the 2x4 was LeLe. She was panting and looking down at her victim like he was a piece of shit. Abruptly, she tossed what was left of the 2x4 aside.

"Y'all ok?" LeLe asked, stepping over the body to them.

"Yeah, we're ok," Yada confirmed with a smile, happy to see her best friend. They hugged one another.

"How's your arm, bro?" LeLe asked, studying the gunshot wound in Voss's arm. A crimson stain had expanded on the sleeve of his shirt.

"I think it's just a flesh wound. I should be straight." Voss reported as he examined his wounded arm. He then walked over to the nigga that LeLe had just clocked over the head with the 2x4. Kneeling down to him he pulled off his ski mask. He didn't know the Mexican man lying at his feet, but he was sure he was connected to Boss Dawgs Outlaw Gang, which was one of the biggest Mexican street gangs in Southern California. Yada and LeLe stood side by side. They watched as Voss lifted up the black thermal the man was wearing, and then his left sleeve. The girls exchanged curious glances, wondering what Voss was doing.

"What are you looking for?" Yada inquired.

"I'm checking for tattoos. I suspect this piece of shit belongs to the other side. All of them have ink that tells their affiliation. Ah, there we go," Voss smiled. He just rolled up the dead man's right sleeve and exposed his tattoo. It was of the George Town Hoyas bull dog. BDOG was beneath it. The tattoo was fading so Voss gathered that homeboy had been down with Boss Dawgs for quite some time. "Yeah, just like I figured. Now, let's check out this one," he walked over to the masked Mexican that he'd taken out when he first arrived on the scene. He checked his body for tattoos. He found that he was wearing the same ink as the first Mexican man he'd checked.

"Both of these fools are BDOG," Voss stood up; holding his arm and looking down at the poor bastard he'd taken out.

Yada walked over to the dead man spitting in his face and kicking him.

Voss turned to her and said, "Shit is really real out here. We've gotta call yo pops so he can clean these fools up and…"

"Oh shit!" LeLe said from where she was standing, eyes cast on the floor. Voss and Yada frowned up. They looked to where LeLe was looking and the man that she'd knocked out cold had disappeared. "Where the fuck could he have gone?" she ran over to the space that the masked gunman was lying, then spun around the living room, looking for him. When she didn't see him, she ran to the door. Voss and Yada were right behind her. They all peered outside, looking from left to right. Homeboy was long gone.

"That nigga gone. Y'all close the door, I'm finna hit up Lyndell," Voss said over his shoulder as he headed to the kitchen to use the telephone that was hanging on the wall. The girls closed the door. They then headed into LeLe's bedroom so she could get dressed.

Voss, Yada and LeLe were chilling on the couch waiting for Lyndell to arrive. When they heard knocks at the door, they looked alive. Yada jumped up from the couch and approached the door, looking through the peephole. Seeing who it was she unlocked the door and pulled it open. She stepped aside and her father, Lyndell, strolled in. As soon as Yada closed the door and locked it, she hugged him lovingly. He kissed her cheek and cupped her face. Looking into her eyes, he asked her if she was ok, to which she nodded yes.

"You and LeLe are gonna stay at my place until I get chu set up at another house. Ok?" Lyndell told his daughter. She nodded. "Ok. Y'all pack y'all stuff while I talk to Voss."

With the order having been given, Yada and LeLe headed off to their respective bedrooms to pack their things. Lyndell walked over to Voss and sat down on the couch next to him, pulling out his cigar and lighting it up. He blew out a cloud of smoke, then returned the Zippo lighter he'd used to light it to the pocket inside of his suit.

"Fill me in, son," Lyndell told Voss. He listened to him as he smoked his cigar, polluting the air with smoke. Voss informed his boss of what had occurred. Once he finished, Lyndell's forehead creased and he looked to the dead man that was left. He then looked around the bedroom for the other nigga, but he didn't see him there. "Well, where's the other cock sucka?"

"He gotta way." Voss told him.

Lyndell sat up on the couch and mashed out his cigar inside of the ashtray on the coffee table. He then cleared his throat with his fist to his mouth, looking to Voss he said, "These mothafucking Mexicans are coming hard at us."

"I know. We're gonna have to smash all of 'em if we hope to win this war." Voss analyzed the situation.

"Don't worry about it. We'll squash Valdez and all of his crew. We May needa call in reinforcements, but they'll get handled."

"What about them Haitian niggaz you deal with? You think they will lend us a hand?" Voss said.

"Yeah, I fucks with that nigga Yee hard. I'm sure they'll lend us some assistance."

"Good."

"Fuck are these two niggaz?" Lyndell pulled back the sleeve of his suit and checked the time on his Audemar Piguet.

"Who?" Voss's forehead deepened with lines.

"Jabar and Bang. They're gonna clean up this mess." He informed him.

Knock, knock, knock, knock!

"That must be them," Voss left the living room to open the backdoor. A moment later he returned with Jabar and Bang. They were wearing navy blue caps and matching jump suits. Verminators was emblazoned across the front of their caps and the right breast pocket. They were posing as exterminators. Jabar was carrying two metal tool boxes while Bang was carrying one. When they walked inside of the living room, they looked over the dead body left for them to dispose of.

"Boss dawg, this it?" Jabar asked Lyndell as he pointed to the cadaver on the living room floor.

"Yeah, that's it. The other one got away." Lyndell frowned up. Then, he looked to Voss curiously.

"No complaints here, just makes our job easier," Bang claimed. He and Jabar sat their tool boxes down and approached the corpse.

"Alright, daddy, we're ready to go," Yada said of herself and LeLe. They returned to the living room with their bags packed.

"Ok."

"What's up y'all?" Yada looked to Jabar and Bang, throwing her head back like *What's up?*

"'Sup?" Bang greeted her.

"What's up, lil' mama?" Jabar smiled at her. He then looked to LeLe. "What up, lil' bit? You not speaking tonight?"

"I'm—I'm sorry, y'all, it's just been a bad night for me so my mind is everywhere. My fault. What's up with y'all?"

"Ain't shit. Onna job," Jabar responded. He then turned to Bang. "Come on, man, help me lift this dead mothafucka up." Jabar grabbed the dead man under his arms while Bang hoisted up his legs. Together, they carried homeboy off wincing as they moved along.

"Ok, ladies, this is how it's gonna go," Lyndell began. "I'm gonna take LeLe to my place, and, baby girl, you're gonna take Voss to the hospital. Capeesh?" he looked Yada in her eyes.

"Capeesh," she replied.

"Good. I'll take yo bags." Lyndell took his daughter's bags and kissed her on the cheek. He then looked to LeLe and motioned his head towards the front door, signaling for her to follow him. She obliged and they headed out of the house, Voss and Yada bringing up the rear.

***

Jabar and Bang drained the blood from out of the dead Mexican's body and dismembered it. They then put the body parts inside of a thick black bag. Using a tool that looked something like a blow drier, they sucked all of the air out of the bag, which sealed the body parts inside of it tightly. Once they stored the bag inside one of the tool boxes, they put on surgical masks and grabbed two tall aluminum canisters that looked like spray can bottles. The chemical these canisters contained would help clean any traces of the dead person's DNA from the scene. Once Jabar and Bang were done, they loaded up the rest of the equipment inside of their tool boxes and made their way out through the back of the house, where their Verminators van was parked. Bang drove while Jabar placed the passenger seat, watching everything around him attentively, while talking to his right-hand man.

"Yo, that bitch Yada bad than a mothafucka, boy! I thought fa sho that was gon' be you back in the day, kid."

Bang smiled. He was full of shit though. He knew good and goddamn well that Yada wasn't checking for Jabar's ass.

"Yeah, lil' mama is fine as fuck, which is why I don't understand why she gave that ol' busta ass nigga, Voss, a chance." Jabar balled up his face and shook his head. His nostrils flared and he clenched his jaws, temple throbbing. He balled his fists, hating the fact that Voss had captured Yada's heart.

This ugly ass nigga really thought he had a chance with that bitch! This nigga is hysterical!

"Don't wet it, my nig. There's plenty of other fish in the sea." Bang patted him on his shoulder.

"You're right. There are plenty of fish in the sea, but not like that one. That one there is gonna be mine. One way or another, you feel me?"

"I feel you."

One day Yada is going to be mine, and so will Lyndell's empire. Mark my words. One day! Jabar thought.

***

Voss was admitted into Martin Luther King Hospital for his gunshot wound when Yada had taken him to the emergency unit. He spent a full seven days recovering from his wound before he was allowed to go home. Yada came to see him every day, and today she had come to pick him up to take him home.

"How ya girl doing?" Voss asked Yada once she entered the room, from talking to LeLe over her cell phone. He was sitting on his bed. He'd just slipped his shirt on over his head, and was now putting on his chain.

"She's good. Still a little shaken up, but she'll be alright." Yada said as she came to stand beside him.

"What's the matter with you?" he looked at her scowling face, wondering what had her in a bad way.

Yada mad dogged, nostrils flaring, lips twisted. He continued to ask her 'What's the matter?' without her responding. Then suddenly, she hauled off and smacked him upside the head.

Smack!

"Blood, what the fuck was that for?" Voss' forehead crinkled and his nose scrunched up as he rubbed his head. He was looking at Yada's ass like she'd lost her god damn mind for smacking him upside his head like that.

"I've been holding that for a week. And it's for being stupid!"

Yada smacked him upside his head again. This time harder!

"What? What I do?" Voss asked with a look of confusion on his face, still rubbing his stinging head. Although Yada was a female she hit like a nigga.

"You jumped in front of that bullet, ya damn fool! Are you crazy or something? You could have been killed!" Yada placed her hand on her hip and shook her head. Although she appreciated him taking that bullet for her and saving her life, she was terrified that he might have died. You see, Yada was feeling Voss, and she'd hate to lose him before she saw just how far things between them would go.

"Shiiit, I'd take three more bullets if I thought they'd get me closer to you," Voss threw that cap at her. For as long as he had a tongue he had something smooth or slick to say. The charming mothafucka had always been a ladies' man. The nigga had more game than Parker Brothers, but he wasn't looking to get into Yada's panties. He was looking to get inside of her heart.

Yada blushed and smiled. It seemed as if Voss always knew the right things to say to get her going. She knew she had to watch herself because she was going to fuck around and end up falling for his fine ass. But then again, the way she saw it, who was to say that *that* was a bad idea?

"Well, check you out, Mack Daddy. You stay with some game to spit." Yada smiled harder. She knew L.A. niggaz stayed trying to Mack a bitch out of their panties, so she wasn't trying to fall for Voss's game, and be another notch under his belt.

"Game?" Voss frowned and jerked his head back. "Baby girl, I assure you this ain't no game I'm spitting at chu. This is real talk right here, you feel me?"

"Yeah, yeah, yeah," she twisted up her lips and waved him off. "I bet chu tell that to all of the girls."

Voss pulled Yada closer to him so she'd be standing between his legs. He then said in a low, deep, masculine, sexy voice, "Only the one I'm trying to have something real with."

A serious expression crossed Yada's face as she threw her arms around Voss's shoulders, staring down into his eyes. She didn't know what it was about him but she had it for him bad. She couldn't get enough of his old thug ass.

"Is that right?" Yada asked, in a voice and tone that matched his. Only hers was feminine.

"Most def," Voss replied. At this time, they were moving closer and closer to one another's lips, moving in for a kiss.

Voss's lips were just about to meet Yada's lips, when she frowned up and turned her head toward the door. She then looked back to Voss and said, "Someone's coming."

Voss pulled her even closer and said, "So, let's give 'em a show."

Yada looked at him and grinned, "Later." She gently pushed him back and walked backward until she found herself up against the counter.

Right then, a gorgeous nurse who was thick in all of the right places, rounded the corner inside of the room. She had two small plastic cups, one contained water and the other contained two pain killaz.

"Heyyy, handsome." The nurse said with a jovial expression as she approached Voss. He'd summoned her earlier because the pain medicine he'd taken previously had begun to wear off.

"Hey, Lissa?" Voss smiled at her innocently. He thought she was fine as a mothafucka, but he wasn't checking for her though. Nah, Yada had his undivided attention.

"Excuse you," Yada slid into Lissa's path of Voss and took the two plastic cups from her. "But I got it from here. I can take care of *my* man myself." She looked her up and down with disgust, adding, "Hmmph." She turned up her nose and gave Lissa's ass her back, totally disrespecting her.

Lissa looked from Yada to Voss who shrugged. "I'll be back with your discharge papers."

"Ok. Thank you." He replied.

Lissa rolled her eyes and shook her head, walking out of the door; she said some shit under her breath. "Lemmie gon' and get up outta here 'cause I ain't got no time for this bullshit."

"Here nigga," Yada shoved the plastic cups into Voss's hands. She had a nasty ass attitude. Her eyebrows were arched and her nose was scrunched up.

"Thank you. Damn!" Voss said with a balled up face, taken aback at how rude Yada's ass was. He threw back the pain killaz and washed them down with the cup of water. He then tossed both cups inside of the waste basket.

"Yo ass already done been shot once, let's not make it a second time," Yada threatened. Still angry, she folded her arms across her bosom and shifted her weight from one foot to the other.

"For what? What I do?" Voss chuckled.

"You was smiling with that bitch while yo' woman standing right here." She said as she approached him with her arms still folded across her bosom.

"My woman, huh?" he cracked a smirk at her, letting her know that he was feeling her being his woman.

"Yeah. Your woman," she said as she stood between his legs, holding the gold tiger's head on his chain in her hand, examining the rubies in its eye sockets. He was holding her at the waist with his good hand, staring up at her beautiful face.

"I like those words you've been using since you've gotten here: my man, your woman. Those are the words that couples use." He was looking at her for a response but she was busy studying his jewelry. Acknowledging this, he tilted her chin upward, so she'd be looking him in his eyes. "Are you trying to tell me we're in a relationship now?"

"Yep. And we'll continue to be in one just as long as you play your cards right." She matched his gaze, letting him know she was as serious as a heart attack.

"Alright. It's yo show, so tell me how it's gon' run." He said to her, rubbing his hand up and down her back before settling his hand on her ample ass.

"You will be loyal, faithful, and treat me like a queen...at all times."

"Fa sho. Well, what am I gonna get outta this?"

"Are these rubies real?" she asked him about the stones in his medallion.

His forehead wrinkled with lines and he said, "Hell yeah. Ya boy don't wear shit fake. Now back to what I was saying 'what am I gonna get outta this?'"

"The same, except I'll treat you like the king that you are." She released his medallion and threw her arms around his shoulders again, staring into his eyes.

"I like that. I like that a lot." A smile spread across his lips.

"Good." She kissed him once, then twice, three times, and then they started making out.

Voss and Yada didn't stop kissing until they heard someone approaching again. When they looked to the door, they found the doctor coming through it. The good doctor exchanged pleasantries with them. He then handed Voss two prescriptions slips, telling him about the antibiotics and the pain killaz he'd written on them.

Once Voss had gotten a clear understanding of his medications, he and the doctor shook hands and the doctor took his leave. Voss tucked the script slips into his pocket and slipped on his shirt with some assistance from Yada. Afterwards, Yada helped him slip on his leather jacket and they made their way for the door, hand in hand.

Tranay Adams

CHAPTER FOUR

When Voss and Yada walked through the door of her house, he led her straight to her bedroom. He shut the door behind them and locked it. Voss then cupped Yada's face and leaned forward, kissing her slow and sensually. While they made out, he gradually walked her back until they bumped into the bed, falling over into it. As they made out, Yada went about the task of unbuckling his belt and slipping his jeans below his muscular, hairy buttocks. He then sat up and pulled off both of his shirts, at the same time, slinging them across the bedroom. Yada pulled off her top as well, revealing the bra she was wearing underneath it. She sat up and unhinged the bra, tossing it aside. Voss placed his hand on the center of her torso and gently pushed her back. He placed kisses down her stomach while his hands were busy unbuttoning her jeans, then unzipping them. When Voss saw her panties, he slipped them off her hips and gently bit into them, sinking his teeth into her soft flesh. Yada shut her eyelids and gasped, holding either side of his head as he drove her wild with anticipation of him eating her pussy.

Yada kicked off her shoes while Voss pulled off her jeans, and then her damp panties. He spread her thighs, and tenderly bit down them, one by one. He then went back up them. Once Voss reached her pussy, he teased her clit by flickering it with the tip of his nose. She squirmed beneath him, and licked her lips, waiting for him to devour her juicy pearl. Voss licked Yada up and down, between the slit of her coochie, finding it sticky wet. He then brought his tongue up, licking up against her clit hard, causing her to jump. Holding her thighs apart, he sucked on her clit, slowly at first, and then adding a little pressure. She gasped loudly, like she couldn't breathe, holding his head tighter, and frizzing up his cornrows.

"Ohhhh, shiiiiit, eat cho pussy, boy! Eat cho motha-fucking pussy up!" Yada whined, squeezing her eyelids tighter and biting down on her bottom lip. She started squirting, splashing Voss's chin and soaking the sheets.

Voss's eyelids were shut and his thoughts were concen-trated on what he was doing, which was bringing his wom-an to an orgasm. "MmmmmMmmmm." He made noises as he ate her out, enjoying the taste of her pussy. He started flicking her clit rapidly and fingering her gooey hole, mak-ing his finger glisten wet.

"Oh, baby, that's it! That's fucking it! Aaahhhh!" Yada called aloud and balled her face tight, wrapping her legs around his head. With her leg wrapped around his head, Yada looked like she was performing a grappling move, like them UFC fighter niggaz. Voss removed his finger. He held her thighs and ate her pussy, slow and passionately, while she clawed at the bed sheets, looking down at him through narrowed eyelids and a wide open mouth. She was acting like he was trying to kill her. "Oh, my God, Voss! What're—what're you doing to me?"

Yada threw her head back against the pillow, burying it halfway into it. She screamed aloud as she squirted more and more. She then bit into her bicep, squeezing her eyelids tightly. Her entire body quivered. At this time, Voss sat up and wiped his chin with the back of his hand. He watched as Yada shook uncontrollably. While she was doing this, he kicked off his sneakers and pulled off his jeans, tossing them into a pile on the floor. He then started stroking his dick gently; it appeared to grow stronger, thicker and fuller, its head throbbing, dripping a clear fluid. Once Yada fin-ished shaking, her legs collapsed on the bed and she started massaging that small flap of meat between her legs, which was her clit. She 'ooow' and 'ooooh' seeing her pussy squirt some more, darkening the sheet with her natural juic-es.

"You ready for this dick, ma?" Voss asked her as he continued to stroke his dick faster and faster. As of now, it was at its thickest and riddled with veins. His shit was long and strong, very masculine looking.

"Yesss, please, I want it. I need it, right now." Yada whined. With that having been said, Voss crawled into bed and grabbed her by her hips, pulling her into him. He forced her legs backwards; she locked them behind her head, putting that fat ass, slightly hairy pussy of hers on display. That meaty mothafucka stood out like a balled fist, jumping like it had a heartbeat. Its pink insides shown as it oozed a clear fluid.

Voss sat back on the balls of his feet, rubbing Yada's thigh and tapping his dick against her clit and pussy, causing it to squirt. She squirmed and her eyelids flickered, eyes rolling to their whites. Voss looked at her blissful face as he slowly pushed himself inside of her tight hole, stretching her out and filling her up. He placed his arms into the opening between her arms and legs and outstretched his legs down the bed, looking like he was in a pushup position.

Voss started off slowly stroking Yada's pussy watching her make the most beautiful ugly faces he'd seen in his life. The more he stroked her pussy, the wetter she seemed to become. Head back, eyelids shut, mouth hanging open, she massaged her clit as he stroked her faster, longer, deeper, harder. With each of his powerful thrusts, Voss's nut sack smacked up against her asshole.

"Ahhhh, fuck, bae! Yo, pussy feel so good to a nigga dick! Damn, boo! You ever give my shit away I'll fucking kill you, you hear me? Huh?" Voss said, face sweaty and riddled with veins. He was tearing her ass up, going balls deep, then pulling out and going all the way back up in her.

"Yes, yes, yes! This pussy all yours, babe! I'm not ever giving yo shit away!" Yada swore, lost in the lustful moment of ecstasy. The bedsprings played their music as Voss pounded that pussy out, causing the headboard to bang up against the wall. Yada's eyelids were tight and her mouth was hanging open. She was trying to scream in pleasure but he was fucking the sound out that ass. "Uh, uh, uh, uh, uh, uh...."

Voss switched it up a little, and started hitting her with circular strokes, going faster and deeper, hitting the bottom of the pussy. That shit was driving her ass mad crazy, her toes were curling and shit, and her pussy seemed to be tightening around his dick. He loved that shit. It pushed her to go harder. He grabbed her by the throat and squeezed a little. Yada loved that kinky shit. She looked down at his dick going in and out of her, watching her shit gush upward, like a water fountain. "Oooooooooh!" her eyes welled up with tears, the dick was feeling so good, pushing in and out of her wet, hot, sloppy pussy.

The headboard was banging against the wall so hard and loud, you would have thought somebody was trying to knock the wall down in that bitch. But the only walls getting knocked down were Yada's because that nigga Voss was beating that shit up.

"Oh, Voss, make it hurt, make it hurt!" Yada called out desperately. She'd never had it so good and wanted more. She wanted to get fucked like this forever.

Voss grunted as he continued to pound out Yada, raining sweat on top of her. His back muscles and ass muscles flexed as he handled his business on top of her. He felt his dick growing sensitive the longer he thrust, causing her pussy to ooze more and more. He was turning her on with his manly moans and mind blowing sex. Although the shit was feeling good to him, he wasn't ready to nut up yet, so he ordered her on top of him. He lay back on the bed, motioning for her to climb on top with both hands. Yada crawled over to him, straddling him and grabbing his dick, aiming it for her entrance. She eased it inside of her gasping, feeling her pussy being filled all the way up.

Yada adjusted herself on top of Voss as she started moving her hips in a circular motion, making his dick brush against her walls. Hearing her man moan, she looked down into his face. It was contorted into a mask of pleasure. She could tell that her sex was good to him. The expression on his face and his gripping her hips was indication of it.

"Mmmmmm, ride this dick, girl!" Voss said in ecstasy, loving the way that his lover felt on top of him.

Yada leaned over and whispered into Voss's ear, continuing to work her hips on him. "This my dick, bae? Huh, tell yo wifey this her shit! Let her know this dick is all mine."

"This dick...this dick is all yours, baby. Put it on yo nigga, sho me what that pussy do!" Voss told her with a mask of pleasure still on his face. With the command having been given, Yada sat up, hands on his chest, meaty buttocks sitting on his hairy thighs. She bent her knees to her chest and bounced on Voss's dick, going up and down. She threw her head back, eyelids shut, mouth hanging open. Her full, succulent breasts bounced up and down while ripples went up her ass, each time it clashed with Voss's thighs.

"Uh, uh, uh, uh, uh, uh, uh!" Yada's face balled up, enjoying that dick up in her. "Awww, baaaaaaaae, I feel it, I feel it up in my stomach!" she whined and made another ugly ass face. Her fingers sunk into the soft flesh of Voss's muscular pecks and she pulled them back. In doing this, she broke his skin and caused small bloody streaks to appear. Voss's face balled up in pain and pleasure. It hurt so good! A white lather built up around his dick and her pussy, running down his shaft and saturating his nut sack.

"Babe, I'm 'bouta nut! Shiiiiit, here I come!" Voss's head bent up from off the pillow and he gritted his teeth, vein bulging at his temple. He squeezed her hips tightly and his large hands imprinted her soft meaty flesh. At this time, Yada was screaming aloud and riding his ass faster and faster and faster.

"Oooooou, I'm coming too!" Yada cried aloud, moving even faster. Before she knew it, she could feel Voss spitting glob and glob of his warm semen into her hot womb. She came right behind him, letting off over and over again. Her entire form shook crazily. She then leaned over into the side of his neck, still shaking. She moaned as he held her in his arms. They were both hot and sticky. "Damn, bae, our first time was off the hook." She looked into his face smiling and combing her hair through his frizzy cornrows. He was looking at her face smiling too.

"Fa sho. You did that, lil' mama," he dapped her up. She then cupped his face. Sticking her tongue inside of his mouth, she kissed him slow, deep and passionately.

A few nights later

"Yo, that concert gave me life." A grinning Voss claimed, genuinely having had a good time with Yada. At the moment he was busy rolling up a blunt for them to chief together.

"That shit was lit, I'm glad you enjoyed it." Yada grinned at him, from behind the wheel of her Mercedes-Benz Kompressor. She'd just driven them from the Jay-Z concert, and now they were headed over to BBQ's to grab a bite to eat and a couple of drinks.

Voss looked up from rolling his blunt. Several lines formed across his forehead and he looked closer through the windshield. He saw a very familiar looking Mexican dude behind the wheel of a GMC S-15 Sierra Extended Cab on gold Dayton rims. The truck was a candy apple red, and had a gold grill, door handles, and bumper. The Mexican nigga was busy nodding his head to 2pac Shakur's *So Many Tears*, and smoking the roach end of a blunt. At that moment the event that took place back at Yada's house ripped back and forth through Voss's mind. And he placed the same face behind the wheel of the truck to the face of the Mexican cat that had escaped Yada's apartment.

"Yo, that's him," Voss said to Yada. He'd just turned around from looking at the Mexican dudes that had walked out of the gas station.

"That's him, who? Who are you talking about?" Yada frowned up.

"The mothafucking Mexican that broke into yo spot that night and tried to kill you."

"Bitch ass nigga." She frowned further. She remembered how he and his partner had terrorized LeLe and shot her man too. The thought of all that had her on one, and she wanted blood, just like Voss did.

"Check this out," Voss pulled his gun from underneath the seat, checked its magazine and smacked it back into its bottom. He then cocked it. "I want chu to pull around this corner right here," he pointed with his finger, showing her exactly what corner he was talking about. "I'ma hop out and eat this bitch ass nigga's face. Just keep the car running so you can peel out as soon as I come back."

"Shit, I'm strapped too." Yada pulled her gun from beneath her seat. It was a .45 automatic. "Why don't we both do this nigga? He shot chu and was tryna kill me."

A smile appeared on Voss's face when he saw his girl brandished her own gun. Her being just as gangsta as him made his heart and his dick swell. That shit turned him on, for real, for real.

"I got this one, ma. Limme represent for the both of us."

She stared in his eyes for a moment, loving the fact that she had a man by her side that was willing to defend her honor.

"All right. You got that." Yada gave him a sweet, gentle kiss. She then pulled around the corner like Voss had instructed her to do. He didn't waste any time jumping out of the whip and throwing his hood over his head, keeping his banga low at his side. He hunched over, and made hurried footsteps around the corner, coming up the sidewalk. He looked to his left and saw the Mexican nigga that had popped him at the bulletproof glass window paying for his purchase and getting some gas. He could actually hear the tail end of the punk mothafucka'z conversation.

"Nah, homie, I said fifteen on pump three!" the Mexican nigga threw up three fingers. The African American attendant cracked a grin and nodded his understanding. He then punched in some keys on his cash register and the drawer popped out. He gave the Mexican dude his change back; he thanked him, and then went on about his business.

Once Voss seen his prey about to walk away from the bulletproof window, he moved in fast to stake his claim on his life. Unbeknownst to him, there was a police cruiser parked down the street, in the cut, cloaked in the darkness of the night. Voss got up close enough to spit on his victim before he came up with his banga.

"Oh, shit!" the Mexican nigga's eyes bulged and his jaw slacked, seeing the deadly end of Voss's gun in his face. He dropped the package of Backwoods he'd just purchased. When he peered into Voss's face, all he could see was his eyes, set against darkness. His eyes looked like they belonged on the face of a demon, red, terrifying and without remorse. The Mexican nigga wanted to make a run for it but fear had paralyzed him, so he was left to deal with fate.

Voss, holding his gun sideways, as he pointed it at him, said, "This for Yada, nigga!"

Bloc! Bloc! Bloc! Bloc!

The Vato's brows furrowed and his mouth twisted in a grotesque manner. He fell to the ground and Voss came up on him to finish the execution. He pulled his hood from off his head because he wanted the mothafucka to look into his face and see who was killing him. The Mexican nigga's eyes bulged with recognition and the events that took place back at Yada's house ripped through his mind.

"Yeah, it's me!" Voss spat and then let his gun do the rest of the talking.

Bloc! Bloc! Bloc! Bloc!

Bloody chunks of meat and broken bone flew out of the Mexican nigga's face. Right after, Voss looked up to see the attendant's face. His eyes were as big as saucers and his mouth was open. He was a pimply face, scrawny kid that was wearing trifocals. Even behind the protection of the thick glass he looked terrified. Voss moved in to blow the lock out of the door and go inside and cap his ass to, but hearing the police car siren so close, changed his mind. He looked up the street and saw a police car coming up fast. That's when he tucked his gun and took off running, bending the corner of the same block that he'd took Yada to stay parked with the car idling.

"Haa! Haa! Haa! Haa!" Voss huffed and puffed, reaching the passenger window of Yada's whip. He hunched over into the window but he didn't get inside. Instead he outstretched his hand, flexing his fingers. "Gimme yo gun!"

"What?" Yada frowned up not understanding his reasoning behind wanting her banga. "For what?"

"If I go witchu, then The Boys gon' fa sho catch up with us! Gimme yo piece and take off. I'ma led them after me."

"No. We can make it! Hop in!"

Voss looked over his shoulder. He saw the blue and red lights flashing closer to where they were, and heard the siren that seemed to be flooding his eardrums.

"This ain't the time to argue, gimme the fucking gun and get outta here!" he outstretched his hand even further inside of the window, flexing his fingers. She allowed her eyes to linger on his palm, trying to figure out if she should give him her gun and try to convince him to hop in again or not. Figuring that she'd best do what he'd told her, she pulled her gun back from underneath the seat and handed it to him. "I love you, now get outta here!" he tucked her gun on his waistline and took off running, wiping his fingerprints off of his murder weapon and depositing it into the gutter. When he glanced over his shoulder again, the ass end of Yada's car was disappearing down another block and that one police car had doubled, heading right for him. "Oh, shit!" he couldn't help saying aloud, before running harder and faster, trying to get the fuck out of dodge. There wasn't any way he was escaping those berry and cherry lights though; they were on him like stink on shit. And they weren't about to let up until they had him in metal bracelets or lying dead.

Voss had taken Yada's gun just in case the police pulled her over. This way she wouldn't get charged for the possession of an illegal firearm. He rather he caught the charge than his boo. He also was going to hold onto the gun in case he had to bang it out with The Ones (the police). That's right; he was going to hold court in the streets before he let them put him inside of a cage.

Hearing the police cars skidding to a stop, Voss looked over his shoulder. He saw police officers hopping out of their vehicles and drawing their guns from their holsters, taking aim at him. At this time, he was fearful of being shot down like a goddamn dog in the streets, so his new found fear added to his stamina and he ran that much faster.

Blowl! Blowl! Blowl! Blowl!

Voss ducked low, with bullets whizzing around him. He ran towards a white house, tossing his gun and grabbing hold of the gate before him. He hopped over it with one hand. As he ran up the driveway of the house whose yard he'd entered, he heard a helicopter high in the sky. He knew it wouldn't be long before the ghetto bird's spotlight was shining on him.

"Shit! Haa! Haa! Haa! Haa! Haa!" Beads of sweat gathered on Voss's forehead as he ran up the driveway. He hopped the fence into the backyard and landed on his bending knees. Looking to his right, he spotted a red Doberman Pinscher headed his way growling angrily. *Shit*, he thought to himself as he ran up a line of cars before him, descended the roof tops of them. He jumped onto a gate and had almost pulled himself over, when his foot slipped. He went to fall to the ground of the yard he was fleeing, when a loose wire of the gate snagged his pants leg. He hung upside down twisting and turning as he tried to free himself. Hearing growling, he looked up to the Doberman coming at him full speed ahead, so he threw up his arm. The angry hound bit down on the sleeve of his shirt and pulled on it, jerking its head from side to side, violently.

At that moment, the ghetto bird came flying up. The sound of its spinning propeller filled the air, as its light shined down upon Voss and the hostile animal. Its illumination was so bright that it made him narrow his eyelids into slits.

"Grrrrrrrrgrrrrrrrrr!" the beast growled, with its nub of a tail wagging back and forth.

"Ahhhh! Fuck! Get this fucking dog, man! Get this dog!" Voss was whipped from left to right as the Doberman Pinscher shook its head.

Boom!

The backdoor was kicked open by a big, fat son of a bitch. He was wearing a black do-rag with the flap in the back, a wife beater, boxers and house slippers. He held up his pump shotgun, racked it up and pointed it in Voss's direction.

"Well, I'll be damned. You stealin' piece of shit, tryna come on my property and take what's mine? That serves yo' ass right." The big man said, thinking Voss hopped the fence to steal some of the tools inside of his garage, like so many other crackheads had done. Satisfied to see that his new guard dog, Diablo, was attacking who he assumed was a thief; he lowered his shotgun at his side. He then threw up his meaty fist and shook it, egging his hound on. "That's it, Diablo, chew his mothafuckin' ass up! Bon Appetit, bon appe-fuckin'-tit!"

While the big man was talking shit and waving his fist, his wife, a fat woman one size smaller than him, came up behind him. Her hair was in pink curlers and she was wearing a purple house coat, and trying to see what was going on from over his shoulder.

"Carl, what the hell is going on out there?" the big woman asked her man, with her chubby hand on his shoulder.

"Diablo caught one of them thievin' sons of bitches that keeps hoppin' over into our yard, stealin' my tools and shit, baby!" he said over his shoulder but kept his eyes on Voss and his dog.

"Grrrrrrrr!" Diablo continued his mauling of Voss, whipping his head around.

"Ahhhh! Ahhhh!" Voss squeezed his eyelids shut and hollered out, punching the dog in the head over and over again. No matter how many times he fired on that goddamn dog, the bastard wouldn't release him.

Boom!

The gates flew open and the police flooded the back-yard, guns drawn. They made Carl's fat ass toss his shotgun into the grass and get down on his knees. They then hand cuffed him and made him lie on his stomach with the side of his face pressed against the ground.

"Ahhh, fuck, man! These mothafuckin' handcuff are too tight! Fuck y'all doing me like this for? I'm the victim here! I'm the victim here! That mothafucka trespassing on my property!"

"Shut the fuck up!" one of the pale skinned, blue eyed cops barked down at him.

Carl's eyes shifted over to his Doberman pinscher, still mauling Voss's ass as he hollered aloud. The rest of the police officers were moving in on the dog with their guns on him, beaded to kill.

"Call 'em off! Call 'em off or we'll be forced to put 'em down!" another one of the police officers said to Carl.

"Fuck you mothafuckin' crackas! Sicc 'em, sicc dem mothafuckin' white devils, Diablo!" Carlo called out to his loyal hound. At that moment, Diablo turned around to the cops with a bloody mouth, growling. "Sicc 'em, boy!"

With the order given, Diablo charged at the cops, and their guns made it sound like the 4th of July.

Pop, pop, pop, pop, pop, pop, pop, pop, pop, pop, pop, pop, pop, pop, pop, pop, pop!

The police officers cut the hound down and left him in a pool of blood and his insides.

"Awwww, you mothafuckaz, you mothafuckaz you! You done killed my baby! You done killed my goddamn dog!" Carl broke down crying and slobbering, tears splashing on the concrete.

"We told your dumbass to call 'em off!" Carl's arresting officer told him, angrily. The ghetto bird flew above shining its bright spotlight on everything and everybody, propeller spinning around noisily.

Three days later

When Voss and several other inmates were taken into Men's Central County Jail, they were made to strip down naked. The corrections officers, who were all wearing disgusted expressions, took the inmates clothing with gloved hands, holding it like it was contaminated. The officers went through the inmates clothing thoroughly, making sure there wasn't any weapons or contraband hidden within them. While this was going on, another corrections officer told them to open their mouths wide, lift up their tongues, and move it around. As Voss was performing this action, a C.O was shining a small flashlight inside of his mouth. The officer made him take down his cornrows and run his hands through his long hair. He then went on to check inside of his ears, and behind his ears. He was then told to lift up his nut sack and pull back the foreskin on his dick. Afterwards, he was made to outstretch his arms, wiggle his fingers, squat, and cough hard, three times. The reason for this was just in case an inmate had anything stashed in his asshole; a deep, hearty cough would dislodge it.

"*Alright, now, turn around, bend over and spread your ass cheeks.*" *The C.O commanded all of the inmates.*

"*What?*" *Voss's forehead creased. He just knew he'd heard wrong.*

The corrections officer took a deep breath and rolled his eyes, annoyed. He then repeated himself. "*Turn around, bend over and spread your ass cheeks!*" *he said a little louder.*

This shit gay as fuck, Blood! Voss thought as he turned around and did as instructed.

"*Now, I want chu to cough,*" *the corrections officers said.* "*Gimme three harsh, deep, resonating coughs.*"

With the command having been given, all of the inmates coughed. Some of them fucked around and farted so it smelled like ass in addition to foul body odors and sweaty nut sacks.

Afterwards, the inmates were told to stand back upright. The C.O. checked underneath their feet and told them to wiggle their toes. Next, they were told to line back up.

"Okay, shit-heads, I want chu to line up, nuts to butts in a single file line." The corrections officer looked around at the faces of the naked men, looking like they were pissed off about having to line up so close in their nakedness. "If any of you fucks are thinking about giving me any shit, I'll jam this nightstick up yo ass and turn you into a fucking popsicle!"

With the threat having been given, the inmates did like they were told. They were led to a shower room where they took care of their hygiene, got dressed in their uniforms, took photos and were given their prison identification number.

Once she was frisked and had her purse searched, Yada was finally allowed entry into the visiting room. Her eyes went down the row of Plexiglass windows where the visitors were sitting on stools and talking on the telephones to their incarcerated loved ones who sat behind the thick, scarred up glass. There was one vacant stool and behind the glass was Voss dressed in a navy blue jumpsuit and wearing an identification wrist band. His forearm, where Diablo had bitten him, was wrapped in bandages. Yada sat down on the stool and picked up the telephone. When Voss picked up his telephone and placed it to his ear, she couldn't stop smiling.

"I got some good news." Voss smiled at her.

"I got some good news too, but chu go first." Yada smiled back at him.

"I talked to my attorney yesterday. He says the witness recanted his statement so they're dropping the murder charge. I just have to do fifteen months for the gun, but fifteen months ain't shit. I can do fifteen months standing on my fucking head."

"Oh, baby, that's great news. You'll be out here with me in no time, then."

"Yep," he smiled broadly right back at her. Hearing that he'd be released soon made his day behind that concrete and steel complex, especially being in there with those sad looking mothafuckaz that were getting the long walk (life imprisonment).

Yada faked like she didn't know what Voss's good news was, but she actually did. You see, Lyndell found out who the eyewitness was at the gas station attendant, and sent Jabar and Bang's ass to his place of employment to see him. Once the poor bastard got off of work they followed him home and blocked his ass in his driveway. They roughed him up and shoved a gun into his mouth, making him promise to change his statement that he gave to the police. Fearful of having his life taken, the scary mothafucka did exactly what they wanted. And the rest is history.

Voss went on to tell Yada where his life savings was inside of his house and the combination to his safe. He wanted her to hold on to his money until he got out for fear that someone would break into his shit and steal it. Hearing that he wanted her to hold his money for him made Yada smile inside. She felt like if he was ok with her holding on to his money until he was released from prison then he must really love and trust her.

"Now, what's your good news?" Voss inquired.

Yada knew that they were speaking on the California correctional facility phones, which were monitored by the jail's staff, so she had to chop it up with him in complex wording. She ended up telling Voss that her father, Lyndell, and Valdez, the shot-caller of Boss Dawgs Outlaw Gang, had squashed their beef. They would split drug territory on the agreement that Valdez would kick up six million dollars to Armiya's family (a million dollars for every year the child was alive).

Voss wasn't feeling Lyndell squashing the beef since they had casualties in the war. Men that had lost their lives defending the empire that they all swore their loyalty to, but the old head was the head honcho of their shit so he was going to roll with whatever he wanted to do. He was a soldier, and that's what soldiers did, follow the instructions of their general.

"Good? Shit, that's fucking great news." Voss smiled at her.

"I know, right?" she smiled too.

For a while, there was silence between them and they sat there staring into one another's eyes. Yada batted her eyelashes and smiled harder, blushing and looking away shyly. Every time he looked at her she seemed to have melted. She didn't quite know what it was about him that made her putty in his hands. But she liked it. Nah, she loved it.

"You know, that night that you confessed your love for me. Did you mean it?" she looked him square in his eyes.

"Umm huh," he nodded. "Do you love me back?"

"Yes."

"Yes," he mocked her feminine voice and batted his eyelashes like she did.

She smacked her lips and blushed, saying, "Shut up!"

"Limme ask you something," he started off. "I know we haven't been down with one another that long. But the way things have been between us since we've become official seems so right. I cannot help wondering, if I was to propose to you right now, what would you say?"

"Maybe you should propose and find out, handsome."

Voss opened his mouth to say something, and that's when the corrections officer called for visiting time to be over. With the call given, Yada told her boo she loved him and kissed the glass separating them, leaving a red lipstick imprint behind. Voss kissed two of his fingers and touched the glass. He then hung up the telephone and rose to his feet, getting in line. At this time, inmates was rising from their stools and walking towards the door to leave. An inmate named, Swole, strolled up as Yada was hanging up the telephone. They locked eyes. Swole was a big ass six-foot-three nigga, with a body covered in muscle. The mothafucka was jacked. He looked like he'd fit perfectly fine in body armor, wielding a sword and shield, in the gladiator arena alongside Russell Crowe. His hair was parted down the middle and braided into two little ass pigtails. He wore glasses and had a thick ass goatee that showed signs of graying.

"Say, baby," Swole began. "Next, time you come up here, holla at cha boy, Swole. This dick I got in these draws will set that ass right. I'm every rich woman's fantasy and every poor woman's dream. If you know what I mean," he stuck his long, wet tongue out of his mouth, curling it and uncurling it, demonstrating how he'd be eating her pussy if given the chance.

Hearing his woman being disrespected, Voss whipped his head around as he walked on line. His face was balled up in a mask of pure unadulterated hatred and his jaws were clenched tight. He balled his fists so tight that the veins in them bulged. He wanted to beat the brakes off of Swole's big ass but he didn't want to catch an extra charge and wind up in the hole, so he stayed his hand and formulated another plan of attack in his head.

Yada twisted her lips and shook her head, holding up the middle finger to Swole as she turned to head out of the visiting room.

"That's what I'm hoping for, baby." Swole stated and chuckled, displaying a mouth with half of his top row of teeth missing.

I'm finna try to kill this nigga! Voss thought as he disappeared through the door.

***

Yada made her way up the steps of Voss's home. She lifted up the *welcome* mat and picked up the house key. She unlocked the door and stepped inside. A spear of light cut through the living room and dawned on the sofa. She stood in the doorway taking in the décor of the living room. There was a 55-inch 4K flat screen television set, a brown leather sofa, black carpeted floors and a brown wood coffee table with a smoke black glass top. African masks, spears, daggers, and clothing lined the walls. A life-like statue of Chaka Zulu stood in the corner enclosed in glass with lights shining on it.

Yada nodded her head in the approval of the décor of Voss's home. She then closed the door behind her and headed down the corridor towards his bedroom. She pushed her way inside and flipped on the light switch, opening the closet door. The light bulb that dangled from the ceiling came on when she pulled its drawstring, giving the space life. She got down on her knees and felt around on the floor of the closet, until she found what she was looking for, then peeled a flap of the carpet back and exposed a black iron digital safe. A tiny green bulb beeped and flashed after she entered the combination on the keypad, then the door popped open. Yada pulled the door open and smiled at the blue faces stored inside, then unzipped the Louie V duffle bag she'd brought along and opened it. Yada dipped her hand inside of the safe and removed the stacks, one by one. By her estimation, the amount of money that was there with each band that she dropped into the duffle bag was $300,000 dollars. Once she'd cleaned the safe out, she closed the door and dropped the flap of carpet on it, making sure to smooth the flap of carpet out so that it would blend in with the rest of the carpet surrounding it, before turning out the light and leaving the bedroom.

CHAPTER FIVE

"Fuck you doin', Blood?" Brain asked Voss, seeing him drop a lock inside of a sock, and test swinging it against the top bunk. He was swinging the 'slock' aka lock in a sock hard as hell against the mattress, causing it to deflect off of it.

Brain was a six-foot cat of a brown hue. He rocked a fade with deep 360 waves and glasses to correct his vision. He was an average student at best in school. And he'd only gotten the name, Brain, because the nigga looked smart as shit wearing his glasses.

"Finna set a fuck nigga straight right quick. I'ma need you to watch my back." Voss wrapped the sock around his fists and did a few more test swings against the bed before he figured that he was ready.

"Fa sho', you know I got chu faded. Who head you on though?"

"Swole. Nigga disrespected my queen while I was on a visit."

"Whenever you ready."

"Let's roll."

Voss walked out of his cell with Brain bringing up his rear. Brain stayed a safe distance away from his comrade so it wouldn't look like he was walking with him. His homeboy was about to lie down a hit and he didn't want his involvement to be acknowledged. When Voss walked inside of Swole's house, he found him sitting on the bottom bunk, flipping through a Don Diva magazine. A shadow invaded Swole's space. He looked up just in time to see Voss swinging the sock into his face, breaking his nose. The impact of the sock sent blood flying, staining the inside of the magazine with dots of blood. When Swole grabbed his face, Voss didn't let up on his ass; he struck him over the head, again and again. Each blow sent more blood flying, dotting the floor and walls.

A bloody faced Swole tried to grab Voss's leg but he moved out of the way, cracking him in the back of his skull. Once that big nigga fell on his hands and needs, dripping blood, Voss stepped over him and looped the sock around his neck. Voss used the sock to strangle him, pulling it as tight as he could, chocking his ass out.

"Gaaagagagaga!" Swole's eyes looked like they were about to pop out of his head. He tried reaching up to gouge out Voss eyes, but Voss kept moving his face from left to right to avoid him. Beads of sweat gathered on Voss's forehead and dripped off of his brow, splashing on the concrete floor.

"Ho ass nigga! I'ma mothafucking savage, fool! You shoulda known notta come at my queen like that! But chu gon' learn! Oh, yeah, yo big ass is gon' learn today!" Voss held the sock around Swole's throat with one hand. He then bit down on his bottom lip and punched Swole in the back of head with all of his might. Once he figured that he was barely conscious, Voss let him go and he slammed face first into the slab, busting his forehead. He moaned weakly in pain. Voss then kicked him in his side twice and then in his temple. He looked to the door and Brain was still watching out, looking from left to right.

Voss rifled through Swole's cell until he came up with his cellular. He wiped the sweat from off his forehead and slung it to the ground. Placing his foot onto Swole's back, he said, "Now, I'm finna call my lady, and yo bitch ass is gon' apologize. Ain't that right, big man?"

"Yeahhhh." Swole said hoarsely, looking like he'd gone a few rounds with Mike Tyson.

Voss dialed up Yada. "Heyyyy, baby, what chu doing?"

"I just left yo house. Now, I'm on my way home. What jack you calling me from?"

"My new cell phone."

"New cell phone, huh? Yo ol' thug ass, who you done jacked for that?"

He chuckled and said, "You wild, girl. My nigga friend limme have this."

"Yeah, right."

"Anyway, you know ol' boy that holla'd at chu before you left from seeing me today?"

"Yeah, how could I ever forget that asshole?" she said, sounding like she'd gotten an attitude even hearing about Swole's ass.

"Well, he'd like to apologize for the way he was acting."

"For real?" she sounded surprised. "I'm shocked, bae. 'Cause dude don't seem like the type to apologize for shit."

"Well, my friend Swole seems to have a change of heart. My nigga has seen the error in his ways." He assured her. "Limme put 'em on the line."

With that having been said, Voss whispered into Swole's ear what he wanted him to say to Yada. He then placed the cellular to his ear, listening to him say, "I'm...I'm sorry for what I said to you earlier, beautiful black queen. It will never hap-happen again."

"Hello?" Voss came back on the jack.

"Voss, baby, why does he sound like that? What chu do to him? You don't needa be doing nothing in there that'll get more time tacked on to yo sentence."

"I'm hurt that chu would think I'd risk doing something in here that would delay me getting back home to you. I really am." He said, acting like he was truly heartbroken. "This man has just gotten dental work done. That's why he sounds like that. Now say you sorry."

"Oh, well, I'm sorry, baby."

"Apology accepted." He told her. "Look, I gotta go. I'll get witchu later tonight. I love you, ma."

"I love you more. Muah!" she disconnected the call.

Voss stashed the cell phone in his pocket. He then grabbed a bag of commissary that was secured in a green net fabric. Coming out of Swole's cell, he passed the bag of goods to Brian for his part in the assault and they headed back to their cell. While in their cell, Voss made a few more calls, putting together something really special for his queen, Yada.

***

Yada killed the engine of her Benz Kompressor and hopped out of it, slamming the door shut behind her. She made her way across her front lawn, looking down inside of her purse and rifling through it for her house keys. Pulling them out, she shuffled up the steps and to the front door of her home. As soon as she opened the door she slowed her stroll, slowly pulling the door shut behind her. Yada was taken off guard when she saw LeLe standing before her with a big ass bouquet of the loveliest red roses she'd ever laid her pretty eyes on. All of the lights were out in the living room. The only light was the burning logs inside of the fireplace. Besides that, there were the long, thick candles burning at the center of the kitchen table on top of table cloth. There were also silver domes sitting at opposite ends of the table which covered plates of food.

What the fuck is going on here? I hope this bitch ain't finna tell me she on some gay shit 'cause I'm strictly dickly.

A frowning Yada locked the door behind her and tossed her purse on the end table, which caused her black tube of lipstick to slide out of it. She then hung her keys on the key rack beside the door. Yada then turned around to find a smiling LeLe approaching her. She looked at her questioningly, a frown upon her face as she took the bouquet of flowers into her arms.

"Girl, what's this? What's going on?" Yada questioned her as she turned the roses up and inhaled their scent 'causing a smile to spread across her lips. She shut her eyelids briefly and inhaled the wonderful arrangement again. Yada was the typical girl. She just loved flowers, chocolate and romance. It was safe to say that she was a sucker for all three.

"You'll know everything you need to know in a second, sis. Just gimmie a minute," LeLe said as she held up one finger and *Facetimed* someone through her iPhone 8. A moment later, that nigga, Voss's face filled up the screen, and she held the cell phone out to Yada. "Here she is, bro."

Yada switched hands with the bouquet and took the cell phone, forehead creasing. She couldn't help wondering who her homegirl had hit up. When she laid eyes on Voss she couldn't stop smiling, and neither could he.

"Baby, you know a nigga love you to death. You all a nigga want and need. I can't see myself being with any other woman in this lifetime..." As Voss went on talking, Yada's eyes turned glassy because she realized then that he was proposing to her. Her vision became blurred like she was looking through crystal. "Kenyatta Marie Combs, will you marry me and make me the happiest man on earth?" Voss spoke from where he was down on one knee. He wasn't holding up a ring, but once she looked up, she saw LeLe down on one knee. Outstretched before her was the most beautiful four karat ring she'd ever laid eyes on. It was a platinum band. With a square pink diamond at its center and was surrounded by smaller canary yellow stones.

"Oh, yes, yes, baby, I'll marry you," Yada called out. Her eyes instantly watered. With the answer having been given, LeLe, with tears in her eyes, held her homegirl's hand and slid the engagement onto her finger. Yada stared at her ring admiringly, astonished at how fabulous it was.

The diamonds in the gold band gleamed under the soft lighting of the room.

"Blood, she said yes," A smiling Voss looked over his shoulder at Dough Boy. He was a six-foot-three, three-hundred-pound nigga. He had skin the color of onyx, a big bald head and a body of solid muscle. The mothafucka was built like he wore a cape and fought crime.

"Congratulations, my nigga!" Dough Boy came from behind his back with a golden bottle of Ace of Spades, shaking it up. He popped the top off the mothafucka and champagne suds flowed over his knuckles. Dough Boy sprayed Voss's face with the champagne and dumped some of it on his head, splashing it. Voss laughed and swiped the alcohol from out of his eyes. He then turned to Dough Boy and they slapped hands, hugging each other. They rocked back and forth. Voss then broke their embrace and patted Dough Boy on the shoulder.

Voss took the time to dry himself off, and focused his attention back on Yada. At this time, LeLe had popped open her own bottle of Ace of Spades and poured her girl up a drink in a champagne flute, passing it to her.

"Thank you," Yada accepted the glass. Her stomach was fluttering with butterflies, and she was too anxious to see what else her fiancé had up his sleeve to drink.

"You welcome, boo." LeLe sat the sweaty bottle of Spades back where she'd picked it up from.

"Yo, Treasure, hit it!" Voss called out.

"Treasure?" Yada's forehead wrinkled with lines as she looked around curiously, wondering who Voss was talking about because she and LeLe were the only ones who'd entered the apartment. Right then, someone began playing the grand piano behind her and LeLe. She turned around, and her eyes nearly leaped out of her head. Tears started pouring down her face in buckets right then. She found the R & B Princess Treasure Gold. Her hair was pulled back in a bun and she was wearing a Chinese bang. The diamonds hanging from her ears were dripping, resembling chandeliers. The midnight blue dress she was wearing was sheer. It had ruffling around its collar and at the end of its skirt.

Treasure was sitting at the bench before the piano. Posted up beside her was a big ass muscle bound nigga, with a meaty head that had gang tattoos on it. He was decked out in a light gray suit and black leather slip-ons. From the look on his face, Yada would have sworn he'd never had a good day. But then again, she supposed it was his job to look like a Billy Badass being that he was paid to protect one of the biggest superstars in the world.

Treasure looked at Yada and smiled, boasting her pearly white teeth, as she played the sleek, black piano, covering Treasure Legend's song 'All of Me'.

Yada smiled back at her as tears dripped from her eyes. She was surprised she hadn't notice Treasure, who was her favorite R & B artist, when she and LeLe had arrived. She figured he must have been hiding somewhere in the cut.

'Cause all of me
Loves all of you
Love your curves and all your edges
All your perfect imperfections

By this time, LeLe was taking the roses from Yada and placing them inside of a vase of water, placing it on the dining room table. She was in tears too. She wiped her eyes with the back of her hand, sniffling. Little mama was happy for Yada, and hoped that one day she find a man like Voss that would come and sweep her off her feet.

Give your all to me
I'll give my all to you
You're my end and my beginning
Even when I lose, I'm winning

'I love you' Yada mouthed to Voss as she continued to listen to Treasure sing and play the piano. He mouthed it back and smiled. She kissed her palm and blew him a kiss. LeLe came to stand beside her, patting her eyes with Kleenexes and handing Yada some tissues of her own.

Once Treasure wrapped up the song, the girls applauded her. The superstar then approached them, giving them hugs and conversing a little bit.

"Baby, how did you manage to get Treasure here to serenade me? It must have cost you a fortune." Yada asked her fiancé as she looked at his face on the screen of the cellular.

"It was a favor, babe. Me and her hubby, Voss, go way back." He held up the side of his arm. On his forearm, inked, was 230 which symbolized an alliance between 30s Pirus and Outlaw 20s Bloods.

"That's right. Voss and my boo go back to the sandbox." Treasure smiled.   "Say, Treas, I know you've gotta be going but do you think it would be too much trouble if I could get chu to sign a few things for me and my girl?" Yada asked humbly.

"Oh, please say, yes. Please, say yes." LeLe pleaded with her fingers interlocked.

"Of course. Not a problem. I'd be glad to." Treasure rifled through her purse for an ink pen while the girls went off to get the items that they wanted her to put her autograph on. Once Yada and LeLe returned, Treasure put her Treasure Hancock on their memorabilia. She then gave them both a double cheek kiss, said goodbye to Voss and made her exit. Afterwards, LeLe said goodnight to Voss and Yada with a hug before retiring to her bedroom. This left Yada and Voss alone to enjoy their respective dinners.

One week later

Yada, Lyndell and LeLe's passage through the prison went smoothly, until Yada tried to go through the metal detectors. Yada went through the metal detector a total of three times, and all three times the machine's alarm sounded off. This was due to the hairpins in Yada's hair, the jewelry around her neck and wrists and the wiring her bra was made out of.

After Yada removed everything that caused the metal detector's alarm to sound off, she stepped through the machine without a hitch. Right after, male and female corrections officers thoroughly patted her, LeLe and Lyndell down. With that out of the way, a stock Asian corrections officer with a shaved head and a slight build, escorted them to the visiting room where the wedding was to be held. Walking down the hallway, an excited Yada interlocked her fingers with LeLe and her father, Lyndell. Lyndell smiled at her and lifted her hand to his lips, kissing it.

"This is my baby girl's big day," Lyndell smiled proudly.

"Yes it is, thank you so much for coming, daddy." Yada kissed her father on the cheek and he blushed.

"Of course, I wouldn't have missed it for the world." He swore to her.

"Oh, my God, I'm so happy and excited for you, Yada." LeLe, wearing a big ass smile on her face, jumped up and down excitedly.

"Thanks for coming, girl."

"You ain't gotta thank me. You've been my ace since third grade. You know I'ma hold you down. You just make sure you come to mine."

"I'll be there with bells on."

"You had better, bitch!" LeLe's eye bulged and she smacked her hand over her mouth when she saw Lyndell eyeballing her for cussing. He raised his left eyebrow and tilted his head downward like *Your ass know better than to be cussing in front of me.* "Oops, my bad, Mr. Combs."

"Right this way," the Asian corrections officer said, turning to walk inside of the visitors' room. At that moment, Yada broke off from LeLe and Lyndell. The biggest smile spread across her face once she laid her pretty brown eyes on Voss. Voss returned the smile that his bride presented him with. Homie wasn't wearing a suit, but he was still fresh to death. Well, as fresh as any nigga could be in his state penitentiary issued attire. Voss's hair was braided into six neat cornrows, and his facial hair and goatee outlined his jaw and mouth perfectly. His sky blue shirt and blue jean pants, both of which had CDC imprinted on them, were pressed and creased. They looked like he'd gotten them out of the cleaners.

Yada could tell he had been working out too. He was twice the size he was before he'd gotten locked up. He looked as if his muscles had gotten muscles, and he had fresh tattoos on his neck and hands. Yada made note of the additional red tattoo tear which was below the original two he already had underneath his right eye. This let her know he'd put in some work while inside, which concerned her. The last thing she wanted was for the state of California to take her husband away from her before she'd gotten the chance to experience what it was like to be married with him on the outside. With that in mind, she made a mental note to holler at him about his activities while he was behind the wall.

Voss was smiling from ear to ear when he laid his eyes on Yada. He'd always thought she was attractive. But in that moment you couldn't tell him that his boo wasn't the most beautiful woman in the universe. There wasn't anyone on the planet that could convince him otherwise.

"Hey, my King," Yada smiled and took Voss's hand, placing her platinum band into his palm and closing it.

"Hey, my Queen," Voss smiled back at her. She shut her eyelids and tried to kiss him, but he placed his hand on her shoulder, stopping her. Instantly she peeled open her eyelids, wondering what the problem was as a crease formed on her forehead.

"What's the matter, baby?" she questioned him with concern.

"Hold on to that kiss, lover. I want our next kiss to be as a married couple." He grinned.

Yada grinned back at him, blushing. Her cheeks had turned a rose pedal red. She was absolutely smitten by her husband to be.

Voss glanced down at the platinum band, looking inside of it to see if Yada had gotten exactly what he had wanted engraved in it. She had. My Wife. My Life. My World. He smiled happily seeing it. The platinum band that Yada had for Voss had Forever Yours and her initials K.C.

"Baby, you got me up here being rude," Yada playfully pushed Voss as she noticed his homeboys posted beside him. "What up, Dough Boy? What up, Do Dirty?" Yada dapped up her fiancé's homeboys. She knew Dough Boy more so than she knew Do Dirty because he was Voss's cell mate. When she'd be on the jack with Voss she'd always hear Dough Boy in the background smoking weed and kicking prison politics with whomever. And as far as Do Dirty, that nigga stayed trying to get her to hook him up with one of her homegirls.

"Ain't shit. I'm just waitin' to see my nigga here make an honest woman outta you." Dough Boy smiled and nudged Voss. He was a five-foot-nine, chubby light-skinned nigga with a nasty scar on the side of his neck he'd gotten in a bar fight. The scar bulged out the side of his neck, looking like a leech, because he'd neglected to seek medical attention. You see, Dough Boy unknowingly made the mistake of trying to holler at some drunken asshole's wife one night at a bar, and the bastard busted a Budweiser bottle on the side of his neck. The dude was rewarded with a broken jaw and arm, but he left Dough Boy scarred for life.

Dough Boy was currently in the pen wrapping up an aggravated assault charge. He'd stabbed a nigga in the ass he'd gotten into an argument with over a parking space at a night club.

At this time, Voss was busy exchanging pleasantries with Lyndell and LeLe.

"That's what's up. I'm ready to get this show on the road, just as soon as the priest shows up." Yada assured him.

"You got butterflies in yo' stomach, huh?" Do Dirty asked Yada with an easy grin. He was a brown-skinned dude that rocked a hairnet. He had shifty eyes, a big nose and small lips. His upper body was muscular and he was strong as shit. He was paralyzed from the waist down and strapped to a wheelchair. He'd gotten the name, Do Dirty, from all of the dirt he'd done in the streets.

Do Dirty had a reputation in the streets for putting in work. Niggaz knew him for playing with guns. He was a gangsta, so he knew he was destined for the graveyard or the penitentiary. Either way, Do Dirty was ready for which ever outcome. But nothing could prepare him for when his wife caught him having an affair, and shot him in the back. After she popped him, she killed his mistress and turned the gun on herself, blowing her own brains out. When the police arrived on the scene, they found Do Dirty lying on his stomach in bed, among bloody sheets, alive but unable to move.

The police searched the house and found a quarter pound of weed and a loaded 9 millimeter handgun. Needless to say, once Do Dirty had gone through surgery, and his wound had healed, he was being shipped off to Men's Central county jail to face trial.

Do Dirty was a convicted felon in possession of an illegal firearm. So he got a dime flat. They couldn't prove the weed was his so the D.A through that shit out. But the gun had his finger prints all over it.

"Yeah," Yada answered with a smile. "I'm anxious and excited to marry this big head dude, all at the same time." She threw a glance in Voss's direction.

"Which head you talking about, babe?" Voss chuckled, referring to the size of his dick-head.

Yada turned red with embarrassment and looked to her father. He hadn't heard Voss though. He was too busy chopping it up with one of the corrections officers. Yada turned back around to Voss and shoved him playfully, talking to him through her clenched jaws, stomping the floor. "Babe, watch yo mouth. You forget my daddy is here?"

Voss smirked and looked in Lyndell's direction, seeing that he was busy talking to one of the corrections officers. "OG, can't hear me from over there."

"Still, watch cho mouth." Yada gave him a look like *Don't make me show my ass up in here.*

"Check baby out, getting all gangsta on her nigga. You got it, boo." Voss assured her.

"I'm sorry I'm late, but I had something to eat that didn't agree with my stomach." A deep baritone voice came from beside Yada and Voss. When they looked they found a stocky, middle-aged African American man. His complexion was damn near that of a Caucasian man, but he had the traditional Black man's features. A broad nose and full lips. He was wearing one of those little beanie-looking hats like the pope, which was called a zucchetto, and a black Roman cassock. The sleeves of his holy garment covered half of his hands. He was carrying a worn black leather Bible with a gold cross on it.

"Oh, don't worry about it, Father. Thanks for accepting this ceremony. This is truly the happiest day of my life." Yada told him.

"You're welcome. I'm sorry, but I seem to be getting forgetful in my old age, what is your name again?" The priest inquired as he shook her hand.

"Oh, I'm Kenyatta Combs. And this is my fiancé," she nodded to Voss. "Voss. Voss Purdy."

"I'm Father McAllister; it's a pleasure to meet chu both." He turned to Voss and gave him a firm handshake, to which he nodded.

"Pleasure to meet chu as well, Father." Yada responded.

"Pleasure to meet chu too." Voss said to him.

"Great," Father McAllister said. "Shall we carry on with the ceremony?"

"Yeah, gimmie one second, Father." Yada turned around and called her father over. He'd just finished programming the correction officer's number into his cell phone, and sliding it back inside of his suit. He then shook the officers' hand and made his way over to his daughter. He and LeLe posted up on Yada's side, while Dough Boy and Dirty stayed on Voss's side.

Voss and Kenyatta stood facing one another, holding hands. You could tell by the looks etched across their faces that they were madly in love with one another.

Once everyone was present and accounted for, Father McAllister went on to perform the marriage.

"Dearly Beloved, we are gathered here today in the presence of these witnesses, to join Kenyatta Marie Combs and Voss Dominic Purdy in matrimony commended to be honorable among all; and therefore is not to be entered into lightly but reverently, passionately, lovingly and solemnly. Into this - these two persons present now come to be joined. If any person can show just cause why they may not be joined together - let them speak now or forever hold their peace." Father McAllister took the time to look around to see if anyone would object to the lovely young couple getting married. No one objected. He then nodded to the couple for them to carry on with their vows.

"I, Voss Purdy, take you, Kenyatta Combs, to be my wife, my friend, my faithful partner and my love from this day forward. In the presence our family and friends, I offer you my solemn vow to be your faithful partner in sickness and in health, in good times and in bad, and in joy as well as in sorrow. I promise to love you unconditionally, to support you in your goals, to honor and respect you, to laugh with you and cry with you, and to cherish you for as long as we both shall live." Voss told her, finding his eyes growing glassy. He hurriedly blinked back the tears that threatened to spill over the brims of his eyelids. He understood that he was in prison and had to remain a G at all costs, no matter what was going on at the time.

"I, Kenyatta Combs, take you, Voss Purdy, to be my husband, my partner in life, and my one true love. I will cherish our union and love you more each day than I did the day before. I will trust you and respect you, laugh with you and cry with you, loving you faithfully through good times and bad, regardless of the obstacles we may face together. I give you my hand, my heart, and my love, from this day forward for as long as we both shall live." Yada told her husband to be as she held his gaze. Tears were slowly rolling down her cheeks as she stood there smiling. Voss extended his hand and wiped away her tears, staring into her face lovingly.

"I, Voss, give you, Kenyatta, this ring as an eternal symbol of my love and commitment to you." Voss took her by the hand and slid the platinum band around her ringfinger.

"I, Kenyatta, give you, Voss, this ring as an eternal symbol of my love and commitment to you." Yada took his hand and slid his platinum band onto his ring-finger.

"By the power vested in me, I now pronounce you husband and wife. You may now…"

Yada went in for the kiss again and Voss stopped her, holding up one finger. He needed a moment so he could address the priest.

"By the power vested in me, I now pronounce you thug and wife," Voss corrected him, with a slight scowl on his face. His menacing demeanor had The Man of the Cloth kind of shook. You see, Voss was thugged the fuck out, and wanted his wedding to be as G as it can get.

The priest cleared his throat with his fist to his lips and swallowed the spit in his mouth, before continuing, "By the power vested in me, I now pronounce you thug and wife. You may now kiss the bride."

With that having been said, Voss and Kenyatta sealed their new union with a kiss. Their friends and family applauded and made cheerful noises.

"I present to you the newly married couple, Mr. and Mrs. Purdy." The priest added.

A jovial Yada turned around to LeLe and her father, saying, like the woman in The Color Purple, "I's married now!"

LeLe laughed, hugging and kissing her best friend.

Dough Boy and Do Dirty hugged Voss and congratulated him. Father McAllister congratulated him and shook his hand. When Voss turned around from shaking the holy man's hand, he found Lyndell approaching and extending his hand. The two of them shook firmly. Lyndell then pulled him closer so that no one standing around could hear what he was about to say. "This officially makes us family, son. You make sure when you get outta here you take good care of your queen."

"No doubt. You know I got this."

"Now that's what I like to hear," Lyndell smiled and then grew serious. "I love you."

"I love you too." Voss countered, hugging him and patting him on his back.

After the wedding was over, Voss and Yada were given three hours to hang together. They made the best of it. Those hours seemed to fly by, and before either of them knew it, it was time for them to say their goodbyes. Voss and Yada shared an emotional goodbye. In fact, things had gotten so intense that Voss was seriously thinking about breaking out of prison, grabbing Yada and running away to one of those countries that didn't extradite you back to the United States. The only thing that stopped him was the thought of putting the love of his life in danger. Well, that and the fact that he would be home in less than two years anyway.

CHAPTER SIX
Release day

Buzzzz!

The buzzer sounded off loudly. A moment later, the barbed wire gate rolled back, and Voss strolled out, sack of belongings slung over his shoulder. A smile stretched across his face when he saw Yada standing outside of a burgundy Mercedes Benz E-class coupe. The gorgeous vehicle gleamed underneath the rays of the beaming sun which kissed off of it. Yada was far more attractive than the luxury car though. She had put on a few extra pounds so she was a little curvier and thicker than she was before Voss went in. But it was ok, because he loved a woman with a little meat on her bones.

Yada's hair was cut shorter and feathered out at its ends. She wore dark burgundy shades, a dark burgundy spaghetti strap shirt, Daisy Dukes which the pockets hung out of and sandals. The lipstick she wore across her lips matched the color of her shirt. She had French tipped fingernails and toenails and there was a gold jewel in each one.

Damn, my boo is finer than a mothafucka, I'ma fuck the shit up out this nigga when we get home!

Yada held the smile on her face as Voss approached her. He wasn't wearing anything extravagant, but his muscular physique made his clothing look damn good on him. Well, at least she thought so. Voss's hulking form filled out a red tank top, camouflage cargo shorts which sagged off his ass, displaying his boxer briefs, and red high-top All Star Chuck Taylor Converses. Voss was rocking a bald head. He'd grown out a thick, nappy beard. He seemed to have packed on even more muscle than he did before. His body was shining under the sun like he had rubbed himself down in baby oil.

Stopping before Yada, Voss dropped his bag at his feet. He then snatched her up, making her say 'Whoooo!'. Angling her downward, he brought her down to his lips, kissing her deep, long and passionately. They made 'mmmmm' sounds as they kissed, eyelids shut. As they continued to make out, Voss walked her up against the car. Smacking as they kissed, they felt one another's bodies, her enjoying all of his solid muscles, and him enjoying her succulent breasts and bodacious ass. They found themselves growing aroused. Voss didn't know it but his dick was bulging in his shorts and poking Yada in her stomach. He lifted her up and carried her over to the hood of the Benz, laying her down upon it, still making out with her. He slipped his hands underneath her shirt and began fondling her breasts.

"Hold on, babe," Yada said as she stopped kissing her man and slipped his hands from underneath her shirt. "You act like you about to try to fuck me, on the hood of this car, outside of the prison." She smiled at him kinkily.

"I am trying," Voss claimed and kissed her. He was so close to her that he could smell the eggs and bacon on her breath that she'd eaten for breakfast, as well as the Chanel #5 perfume she was wearing. It all turned him on. He wanted her. He wanted her bad as fuck.

Yada laughed hardily. "Ol' horny ass nigga."

He chuckled and said, "You goddamn right."

"Come on, handsome, let's get outta here," she motioned for him to jump into the Benz. She fired up the luxury coupe, just as Voss hopped into the front passenger seat and slammed the door shut. She cranked the volume up on Lil' Wayne's *Visine*, drove out into traffic and sped off. The wind blew inside of the vehicle, ruffling the married couple's hair and clothing. Voss nodded his head to the music with a great big smile on his face. He turned his head from left to right, taking in all of the scenery. When Yada looked at him, she could tell he was happy to be out of prison and able to spread his wings.

"Welcome home, baby," She leaned over and kissed him, keeping one eye on the streets before him. Voss held the side of her face, eyelids shut, kissing her like he'd never be able to do so again. He then broke their kiss, and climbed halfway out of the passenger window. He held his arms in the air, looking like the letter V, smiling. The wind blew harder since the Benz was moving so fast, which in turn ruffled his tank top.

"I'ma free man, baby! I'ma free man!" Voss threw his head back, shouting it over and over again, displaying all of the teeth in his mouth.

Vrooooom!

The Benz raced up the street, leaving small pieces of trash and debris floating in the air. Voss was still hanging halfway out of the window, hands up in the air, shouting. "I'ma free man, I'm freeeeee!"

***

Voss had been dreaming about a Big Mac, strawberry shake and fries since he was given his release date. He made up his mind the night before that that was going to be his first meal when he finally touched the turf. So needless to say, once Yada got off the 405 Freeway, he had her dip off to Mickey D's. He ordered up what he had in mind, but instead of one Big Mac, he got two of those bitchez and smashed them shits out. Once he finished off his shake, he grabbed Yada and they ducked off to the Men's rest room, locking the door behind them. Behind closed doors they sucked and fucked each other to orgasms to monster pro-portions. When they emerged from the bathroom, they were fixing their hair and straightening out their clothes, wearing smiles across their faces.

"Babe, gimme yo keys, I'ma try to drive back to the house," Voss took the keys from his boo, and they headed outside, hand in hand. Once they were back inside of the Benz, Voss fired it up. Gripping the steering wheel, he took a gander at the controls of the car, trying to get reacquainted with how to operate the vehicle. Once Voss felt that he'd gotten himself familiar with how the car operated, he threw it in reverse and looked over his shoulder. He mashed the gas pedal and the Benz lurched forward, nearly driving through the window glass of the McDonald's they'd just left out of. When this happened a white couple looked at them horrified. They grabbed their trays and rose from the table, sitting somewhere far from the window.

"Oh, shit, babe!" Yada's eyes got big and her mouth dropped open, holding her hand to her bosom. Her heart had nearly leaped out of her fucking chest thinking they were about to crash into one of the most famous fast food establishments in the world.

Seeing that his wife was scared shitless, made Voss feel bad. So he leaned over and kissed her on the cheek, telling her that he was sorry.

"Hold on, babe. Gimme a second before you pull off again." Yada told him. She then shut her eyelids briefly and took a deep breath to gather herself. Afterwards, she was like, "Ok, let's go."

"Fuck!" Yada cursed. "That was drive."

Voss threw the car into 'reverse' (for sure this go around) and mashed the gas pedal. The car flew backwards and almost hit a navy blue Ford F-150 pickup, which was pulling inside of the parking lot. The driver of the Ford, a younger white dude in a LA baseball cap, blew his horn like a mad man.

The white dude rolled his window down, and stuck his head out of the window, screaming, "Watch where you're going, you fucking asshole!"

"Sorry again, baby," Voss told Yada apologetically. He kissed her all over her pretty face and hugged her affectionately. While he was doing all of this, the white dude was talking big shit. Having grown tired of homeboy popping shit, Voss popped the trunk and jumped out. The white cat did too, ready to fight.

"What the fuck are you going to do, huh? Huh, motherfucker? I'll kick your fucking ass!" the white stud threatened as he removed his jacket and tossed it onto the hood of his truck.

A mad dogging Voss completely ignored him. He opened the truck of the Benz and grabbed the tire iron, chasing the white dude. The white dude jumped back behind the wheel of his truck, and rolling up the window. Voss didn't give a mad ass fuck though. He swung the tire iron, cracking the driver's window, further and further with each swing.

"Punk ass mothafucka gon' come at me like I'ma ho? Like a nigga ain't just finish doing time onna level foe? You got me fucked up, Blood! On Piru!"

The white dude looked on in shock as he held his cell phone to his ear, having dialed up the police. He watched as Voss climbed onto the hood of his pickup and started whacking the windshield with all his might. A cobweb formed on the windshield, growing bigger and bigger the more Voss struck it with the tire iron.

"Voss, come on! We've gotta get outta here! The police are coming!" Yada called out to her husband from out of the front passenger window. By this time the air had filled with police car sirens that were headed to their location.

At the mention of the police, Voss jumped down from off the hood of the truck. Flipping the tire iron over to the opposite end, he gripped it with both hands and slammed it into the front tire. The tire exploded and hissed, going flat. For good measure, Voss harped up phlegm and spat on the hood of the Ford. He then kicked a dent into the side of it. Next, he ran back to the Benz and jumped in. After he tossed the tire iron into the backseat, he pulled out of the parking lot like a goddamn speed demon.

Vrooooom!

The police car sirens continued to blare loudly.

***

Bang jumped in behind the wheel of his midnight blue BMW 745Li and slammed the door shut behind him. He began looking over the list of alcoholic beverages that Lyndell had requested he and Jabar get when the passenger door opened and his main-man jumped in. Jabar fished out the half smoked blunt from out of the ashtray. He stuck it between his lips and patted himself down for a lighter. Once he found it, he sparked up the blunt and blew out a cloud of smoke.

"Man, it must be like one-hundred different bottles of liquor on this fucking paper." Bang told him.

"You know old head gotta have it all since his fucking favorite is on his way home. Dawg, I swear before God I hate that high-yellow, blue eyed bastard, Voss."

Bang chuckled and said, "How long you been keeping that secret?" he took the smoking blunt away from Jabar.

"Kiss my ass, okay?" he looked at him with a serious look on his face. "How would you feel if a nigga stole yo bitch, and yo position in Lyndell's organization?"

Bang looked at him like he was bat shit crazy, leaning his head to the side. "Nigga, since when has Yada ever been yo bitch? That ho won't give you the time of day. And as far as Lyndell's lieutenant, I can't front, homeboy deserves that. He's been down with the old man longer than any of us has."

"Man, fuck all of that, dawg. I done put in a lotta work for Lyndell, and my spot still not solidified. I feel like a fucking chump. Nigga got me doing all the grunt work for years on top of years. I'm better than that. I'm not some low level street soldier, shit."

"And as far as Yada goes?"

"I was wearing that bitch down. Sooner or later I would have found my way inside of her heart."

Bang laughed and shook his head, saying, "You're one delusional mothafucka, you know that Jabar?"

"Yeah, whatever," Jabar waved him off. He really wasn't trying to hear what he had to say. The only truth he was interested in was his own.

Jabar massaged his chin as a bright idea came to mind. Looking to Bang, he said, "Say I came up with a plan that would change our current positions within Lyndell's organization, would you be down with the program."

"What do you mean?" Bang looked back and forth between him and the windshield.

"What I'm saying is if I came up with a plan that would guarantee me a seat at the head of the table, and you beside me as my second in command, would you roll with it?"

"Hell yeah, I'd roll with. Why? You got something up yo sleeve?"

Jabar smiled mischievously as he rubbed his hands together, saying, "My nigga, I always do."

"Well, you know yo dawg is all ears." Bang smiled mischievously as well.

***

Voss drove through the streets with a frown fixed on his face. He was still pissed off about what had happened back at McDonald's. If he could have had it his way he would have driven the tire iron up that white dude's ass for his blatant disrespect. But unfortunately, he didn't get the chance to.

Yada stared at the side of Voss face as he drove the car. He glanced back and forth between her and the wind-shield, wondering why she was looking at him how she was.

"What's up? What's on yo mind, baby?" Voss in-quired.

"Babe," Yada began, placing his hand in her lap and caressing it. Right then, her touch soothed him. He didn't know what it was but it was something about her touch that calmed the savage that lurked in him. "I don't want chu to take this the wrong way. But I think you should see about getting into an anger management class once you get set-tled out here. I mean, I know that guy back there disre-spected you, but chu took it to another level. If the police would have gotten there before we left, they would have been hauling yo ass back to prison again. And I just got chu home, my love. I ain't even trying to have that. You feel me?"

Voss took a deep breath and thought about what she had said. He then turned to her and nodded. "Yeah, I feel you, boo." He brought Yada's hand to his lips and kissed it. They then kissed.

"Do me a favor, handsome."

"What's that?"

"Make a left at the next main street here," she pointed. "I got something I want to show you."

"Okay." He kissed her hand again, and drove to where she'd instructed him to.

When Voss made the left at the light and drove down the block, Yada pointed at different establishments. There was a barber shop, a salon, a Wing Stop, a Subway and two laundry mats. She then told him to go to Bank of America in Inglewood, off of Crenshaw Blvd. Once they got there, he pulled up and parked, cutting off the engine.

"What chu show me all of those businesses for?" Voss asked.

"I just wanted to show you all of the shit you own." She said it like it wasn't a big deal, staring at her nails.

Voss's eyes got as big as saucers for a moment. He couldn't believe what she had just told him. He looked ahead and then turned back around to her, saying, "So those are all my places? I don't understand. How?"

"I'll tell you in a sec," she picked her purse up from between her feet and sat it in her lap. She then rifled through it until she found the red Bank of America debit card, handing it to him. Voss looked at the card and it had his government name on it. He smiled. For as long as he'd been alive he never had a bank card. Hell, he never even had any credit for that matter. But he was sure his wife had changed all of that since he'd been gone. "Come on. We've gotta get chu a couple of dollars outta the ATM. I can't have my man walking around broke. How would that make me look?"

Voss and Yada jumped out of the car and walked over to the ATM. Yada told him the code to put in once he put the card in. She suggested that he make a balance, and he did. A smile was on Voss's face during the transaction. He couldn't wait to see the exact amount of money his wife had put up.

Once the ATM machine pushed out the receipt, a smiling Yada motioned for Voss to take it. Still smiling, Voss tore the receipt free and looked at it. Once again his eyes got as big as saucers when he saw the dollar amount in the checking account, $4,230,568 dollars.

"Yo, babe, this gotta be a mistake. Look at this shit." Voss showed her the dollar amount on the receipt. Yada shook her head and continued to smile. "For real? This all me? I mean, us?" she nodded. "But how though? You never told me."

"I took that $300,000 dollars that chu left me and I flipped that shit, babe. I flipped that shit so you could have something to come home to."

"This is our empire." Voss said, and looked down at the receipt.

"That's right, baby, *our* empire. We planted the seeds." Yada assured him.

"You planted the seeds."

She grinned and said, "You don't have to worry about anything either. My daddy made sure everything is legit. And any money you make with 'em, we'll clean it through the businesses like I've been doing. We straight, baby. I even got us a mansion out in Calabasas, a 7 series BMW Alpina and a milk white Maybach S650 cabriolet with burgundy leather seats, like you always wanted."

"Damn, ma, you did all of that by yo self?" he asked impressed with all she'd accomplished during his short in-carceration.

"Yeah. Alllll by myself."

"Man, my baby is beautiful, smart, intelligent and business savvy. How'd I get so lucky?"

"How did you get so lucky?" she looked at him like he was crazy. Then threw her arms around his neck, saying, "Nah, handsome, how did I get so lucky?" she kissed him slow and lovingly. Voss balled up the receipt and dropped it at his feet. He then continued to make out with his wife while caressing her body, just like how they do in romance comedies.

"Come on, let's go in here and see about getting you some more money." Yada grabbed him by his hand and led him inside of the bank.

That night

"Damn, pops done moved up in the world," Voss said as he feasted his eyes on the huge estate that belonged to Lyndell. Yada had just entered the enormous golden gates which had the crack king's initials on them. The gates were closing back, and she was now driving around the cobble stoned driveway. The fifteen room mansion had a remarkable resemblance to The White House.

"Yeah, we've both been on our shit since you've been gone. But don't wet it, you'll be jumping back right out there into the thick of things. I talked to daddy and he couldn't wait 'til you came home. He was so excited. He wanted to have you a welcome home party but I told 'em you don't like parties so he nipped it in the bud."

"That's my girl," he kissed her on the cheek.

Yada stopped her car outside of the mansion and killed the engine. She and Voss hopped out and met at the rear of the vehicle, interlocking their fingers and then headed up the stairs. Yada knocked on the door repeatedly but no one came to answer. That's when she pulled her duplicate key out of her pocket, and unlocked the door. When she pushed it open, she and Voss met total darkness.

"Fuck happened? Pops forgot to pay the light bill or some shit?" Voss asked Yada with a frown.

"I don't know. Maybe the power went out." Yada responded.

"Bae, get behind me. I'll go in first in case something is going on," he said, pulling his wife behind him as they entered the mansion. He made his way through the darkness, he and Yada calling Lyndell's name over and over again. Suddenly, the front door slammed shut behind them, startling them.

"Bae, you straight?" Voss asked.

"I'm ok, baby." Yada replied.

Suddenly, the lights came back on inside of the mansion, revealing several people. There was an enormous banner hanging across the ceiling that read: Welcome Home Voss. There were tables loaded with platters of food and opened coolers filled with alcohol beverages and non-alcohol beverages.

"Surrrpriiiiise!"

Voss smiled and looked back at Yada, who looked guilty as hell. When he turned back around, niggaz were shaking up bottles of champagne and spraying Voss with it. He laughed and wiped the sudsy alcohol out of his face. He then took a bottle from one of the guys and took it to the head, guzzling it, throat rolling up and down. Men and women started coming up giving him envelopes filled with dead presidents. When he ended up with too much, Yada handed him a pillowcase and he started loading the envelopes into it. She then took it and stashed it in a safe place. Lyndell welcomed him home with a manly hug and kissed him on the side of the head. That nigga Bang dapped him up and then Jabar approached him.

Voss mad dogged Jabar as he walked in his direction. Jabar cracked a half-heartedly smile, but Voss could see right through that shit. Normally he'd keep a nigga at arm's length that he didn't fuck with. But today was his first day out the mothafucking pen, and he didn't want to turn out his welcome home party. So in this moment he was going to hold his tongue and keep his hands to himself.

"Welcome home, my nigga," Jabar slapped hands with Voss and pulled him in, patting him on the back. He rolled his eyes and twisted his lips. He hated the fact that he had to act like he was mad cool with that nigga Voss. The nigga felt like he'd betrayed himself.

"Good looking out," Voss said unenthused, patting Jabar on the back.

"I gotta lil' something, something for you, big dawg." He pulled an envelope from out of his back pocket and passed it to Voss. Jabar watched him peek inside of the envelope as he thumbed his nose. When Voss looked inside of the envelope it was loaded with single dollar bills, while the envelopes everyone else gave him were filled with one hundred dollar bills. Jabar smiled mischievously, knowing that he'd slighted Voss. Voss's face balled up and he thanked him, tucking the envelope of money into his back pocket. Truthfully, he wanted to grab the dollar bills out of the envelope and smack Jabar in the mouth with it. But he knew that would take their little quarrel to another level, and his welcome home party wasn't the place for that.

Right then, Lyndell seemed to have magically appeared within the crowd of party goers. He wrapped his arm around Jabar's shoulders and motioned for Voss to come here. He told him he'd liked to have a word with him and Jabar inside of his study. Voss nodded.

Voss and Jabar followed Lyndell inside of his study where he motioned for them to sit down before his desk. As they done as he instructed, he went on to ask them if they wanted some D'usse Cognac VSOP. Voss declined while Jabar graciously accepted the offer. Lyndell opened his desk drawer and pulled out a large bottle of alcohol, which had a golden cross on it. He poured himself and Jabar a glass of the brown liquor. Jabar picked up his glass of brown alcohol. Closing his eyelids briefly, he took a quick sniff of it and took a casual sip. Lyndell then put the bottle of expensive liquor away and picked up his glass, sitting down in his executive office chair with his initials etched into the headrest of it, LC.

Lyndell took a sip of the fine alcohol and then sat his glass down on the desk top. His eyes shifted back and forth between Voss and Jabar. They looked to be growing impatient, anticipating what he'd summoned them to his study for. Seeing that he was keeping them in suspense, he decided to spit out what he had on his mind.

Lyndell took the time to light up a cigar and blow out a cloud of smoke. He then closed his Zippo lighter and tossed it upon the desk top. "Now, Voss, you were my second in command, but in your absence, I had to hand your responsibilities over to Jabar." Voss nodded his head as a frown etched its way across his face. He slumped a little in his chair and interlocked his fingers in his lap. "It wouldn't be right for me to demote him since you've come home, so I've come up with a peaceful resolution."

"Oh, yeah, what's that?" Voss asked inquisitively.

"You two will share the responsibilities."

"Share?" Voss frowned up further and sat up in his chair. "OG, I don't need no mothafucking help."

"That's exactly what I told 'em," Jabar threw back the last of the alcohol in his glass and sat it down on the desk top. "All another nigga gon' do is get in the way of me doing my job."

Voss shot him a knowing look and said, "You goddamn right? Look, I appreciate you for holding it down while I was gon', but I got it from here. I don't need your assistance. I was doing my thang out here just fine when it was just me." He looked back to Lyndell and said, "Look, OG, I think it's best that we go back to how thangs were before. I go back to being yo' right-hand nigga, and Jabar your enforcer and bodyguard."

What was said seemed to have angered Lyndell because his eyebrows arched and he bit his inner jaw, saying, "Lil' nigga, you don't run shit here, I'm the HNIC up in this piece, this is my shit!" he jabbed his finger into the desk top. "Don't nobody dictate how I run this shit, but me! You understand that? Now, I said you two mothafuckaz are gon' share the responsibilities, if you don't like it, then you're free to step!"

"Step!" An enraged Voss shot to his feet. His movement was so abrupt that it caused Jabar to reach for his waistline, fearing that he was going for his gun. "That's how the fuck you talk to me, after all the work I done put in for yo' mothafucking ass, old man? I laid down the foundation for this empire; I'm one of the reasons why the business is where it's at today. It was the niggaz I got at and the connects that I found that allowed us to flourish, and this how you talk to me? Like I'm some lil' nigga, some mothafucking peon?" spit flew from off his lips, as he spat words like an AK-47 spat bullets.

"Sit down!" Lyndell told him through clenched teeth, staring at him angrily.

"Stop talking to me like I'm yo' mothafucking child, Lyndell!"

Lyndell shot to his feet and smacked his hand down upon the desk top, furiously, saying, "I said, sit cho black ass down, nigga!"

"Nigga, fuck you!"

Blowl!

Lyndell's eyeballs bulged out of their sockets and his forehead creased with lines, wondering what the fuck had just happened. He looked down and touched his torso, coming away with bloody fingertips. He looked back up at Voss accusingly. His lips peeled apart and a small river of crimson blood spilled out of the corner of his mouth staining his turtle neck.

Blowl! Blowl! Blowl!

Lyndell's body jerked violently as he took three more to the chest and collapsed beside his desk. Voss then whipped around to Jabar.

Jabar's eyes widened and he threw up his hands in surrender, fearful, he said, "Hold up, Voss, don't shoo…"

Blowl!

Fire spat from the barrel and ripped off half of Jabar's right ear. He grimaced and fell to the floor. He pulled his banga out of his waistline and Voss took off running out of the study. Jabar scrambled to his feet, wincing and holding what was left of his bleeding ear. He staggered outside of the study, ear ringing with a bizarre siren, seeing Voss fleeing down the hallway. Jabar pointed his gun and squeezed the trigger, causing the vase at the center of the hallway to explode. Voss ducked and bent the corner running. Jabar went after him, gun leading the way. He clenched his teeth, and dripped blood along the way. His sneakers screeched on the Italian marble floors as he pursued the man that had just blasted on him and his mentor.

"Shoot 'em! Shoot his ass!" Jabar called out to the goons in the living room as Voss ran through them, Yada, LeLe and the rest of the guest inside of the mansion.

"What? What's goin' on?" Bang asked as his forehead creased.

"He shot me and killed Lyndell!"

"Oh, my God, no!" Yada cried out. She and LeLe ran past Jabar and down the hallway, heading towards her father's study.

With the word having been given that their boss had been laid down, Bang and the goons pulled their guns from out of the waistlines, just as Voss was pulling open the door and running out of it.

"Get that mothafucka, man!" Bang called out.

Jabar, Bang and the goons spilled out of the mansion after Voss. They hustled down the steps, and stopped at the cobbled driveway, pointing their bangaz at Voss as he fled for his life. The goons stood as a collective, popping of their guns.

Blocka! Blocka! Bloc! Bloc! Pocka! Pocka! Pocka! Blowl! Blowl!

Flames flickered from the barrels of the goons' bangaz and bullets whizzed through the air, making the night sound like a Vietnam warzone.

"Haa! Haa! Haa! Haa! Haa! Haa!" Voss hauled ass across the lawn, heading for the double gates of the estate. He huffed and puffed, occasionally glancing over his shoulder, beads of sweat forming on his forehead and then dripping off the corner of his brow.

Blocka! Blocka! Bloc! Bloc! Pocka! Pocka! Pocka! Blowl! Blowl!

"Oh shit!" Voss shouted aloud, feeling a bullet fly by his ear. Still running, he touched his ear and looked at it. He was surprised he didn't see any blood, and that it was still attached to the side of his head.

Blowl! Blowl!

Voss ducked his head as low as he could and kept on running, feet looking like blurs he was moving so fast. Slowing his speed as he reached the double gates, he leaped into the air and grasped the bars of the first gate. Sparks flew as bullets ricocheted off of the bars of the gates. Voss reached the top of the gate, hung down by one hand and then let go, landing on his bending knees. Sparks continued to fly from off the gates as bullets struck them. Voss, still running, ducked low and hauled ass.

"Fuck!" Jabar cussed heatedly and swung the hand he held his gun in through the air. Suddenly, he staggered backward, blinking his eyes, partial ear ringing and stinging. He touched it and his fingertips came away bloody.

"Damn, dawg, yo mothafucking ear gone," Bang's face balled up noticing that his main man's ear was missing. He tucked his warm gun on his waistline and looked to one of the goons. "Take my nigga to the 'spital and make sure he gets taken care of." He pulled out a fat ass wad of money and gave it to him to pay for whatever care Jabar needed, because he knew the nigga didn't have insurance." He looked back to Jabar. "Come on, man, lemmie help you get inside of Doodles' car." He threw Jabar's arm around his shoulder and held him at his waist, helping him walk back to the goon he'd mentioned vehicle. Once he'd seen them off, Bang gathered the rest of the goons at the welcome home party and they rolled out, looking for Voss's ass.

CHAPTER SEVEN

Yada pulled her father closer to her and bowed her head, squeezing her eyelids shut. She continued to rock back and forth with Lyndell's lifeless body in her arms. Her body trembled and teardrops fell from her eyes, splashing on her father's bloody clothing. Finally, she looked back up, continuing her conversation with God. "Whyyyyyyy? God, oh, God, oh, God! Whyyyyyyyyyy? Please, don't take him God! I love 'em, I love 'em so, so much!" she bowed her head, kissing her father on the forehead. She then shut his eyelids with a brush of her hand.

***

"Haa! Haa! Haa! Haa! Haa!" Voss continued to huff and puff as he ran for his life. His chest was jumping from his rapid heartbeats, and his knees were aching but he kept on running. Five blocks later he found himself exhausted, and slowed to stop, ducking off inside of an alley. As soon as he entered the trashy path, he heard the clinking of an empty can. When he looked he saw a couple of filthy gray rats sniffing around an empty yellow Dole peaches can.

Voss sighed with relief, wiping the sweat from his forehead with the back of his hand. Sticking his head out of the alley, he looked up and down the block. Holding his hand above his brows, he narrowed his eyelids into slits and peered closely. Ahead he saw that nigga Bang's G-Wagon and a van drawing closer. His heart thudded seemingly louder this time, hearing it beating like a drum inside of his ears.

He knew that he was in a bad spot and it would be best for him to move from where he was quickly. Looking ahead he saw a recreational park, about two blocks north. Voss looked back to where the G-Wagon and the van were coming from. The vehicles appeared to be getting closer, their bright headlights nearly blinding him. Figuring that it was now or never, Voss darted across the street, running full speed ahead to the park he'd spotted from the alley. He jogged inside of the park, and kneeled down underneath the shade of a tree. He was sure Bang and the goons wouldn't spot him where he was holing up at. It was too dark for them to see anything. Hell, he had a hard time seeing them for that matter.

"There them bitch ass niggaz is," Voss said from his hiding place, below the tree. He was breathing huskily. His face was shiny from perspiration. There were sweat stains around the collar of his shirt and armpits. He was exhausted, hot, and sticky.

Voss watched as Bang and the goons coasted down the block looking for him. Just as he thought, they stopped their respective vehicles and hopped out, guns in hand. Bang moved towards the alley, motioning for the goons to follow him.

These ho ass niggaz got me ducking and running like I'ma mothafucking punk or something, Blood. I swear 'fore God if I had my strap I'd get active with these niggaz, on Piru. Voss thought as he clenched his jaws and balled his fist. Veins bulged at his temple and hand.

Voss pulled up the lower half of his shirt and wiped his shiny face dry. Looking back up, he saw Bang and the goons jumping back inside of their rides, driving off. Realizing that it was best that he kept his distance from them, Voss ran further into the park, and disappeared into the darkness.

After a couple more hours of searching, Bang and his goons realized that they'd never find Voss that night. But they vowed to capture him and bring him to street justice in the future.

Four days later

It was a Tuesday afternoon and the sky was lit. The weather was a cool seventy degrees. The sun was shining brightly; its rays kissing off of all the people below. A flock of birds flew high across the sky, making those noises that all birds make, flapping their feathery wings.

Yada was a fucking mess during the days leading up to Lyndell's funeral. LeLe and Jabar tried their best to console her. At first, she seemed to be doing ok, but then she'd fall into pieces all over again. She was so bad off at one point that niggaz were suggesting that she be committed to a psychiatric hospital. LeLe wasn't having that shit though. She knew her girl would be ok. She just needed time to heal and a shoulder to lean on.

Since Yada was so distraught, LeLe had to take care of Lyndell's funeral arrangements while Jabar made sure everyone knew where the ceremony was going to be taking place. Everybody and their baby momma came out to pay their respects to Lyndell. That nigga, Jabar, who was wearing a thick bandage over his ear, thanks to Voss shooting at him, made sure that everybody from every gang, triad, mafia and street organization you could think of was there. And it wasn't just because it was Lyndell's last who-rah either. Nah, he wanted those mothafuckaz to know that since Lyndell was dead that he was going to be running the show now.

Yada stood among LeLe, Jabar and Bang. Her eyes were focused on the white coffin her father was enclosed in, with dozens and dozens of red roses on top of it. At that moment she knew this would be her father's last day above ground. The thought of that brought a great sadness to her. She'd made it through Lyndell's wake, but when it came to the burial at the cemetery, she had a hard time controlling her emotions. Sadly, her sorrows got the best of her.

"Nooooooo!" Yada screamed aloud, with spit flying from off her red lipsticked lips. Her pink eyes were wide and streaming tears. Yada's pained scream grabbed everyone's attention attending the funeral. Their brows furrowed and they looked on in awe, watching her run towards the coffin. Yada smacked all of the red roses from off the coffin, sending petals and roses flying everywhere.

The minister, a great, big fat black man in glasses, clutched his Bible to his chest. His eyes were wide and his mouth was hanging open. He looked at Yada in her craze, wondering when someone was going to stop her.

"Don't leave me, don't leave me, daddy! I can't be without chu!" Yada cried, tears flowing rapidly down her cheeks, causing her face to shine. She smacked the last of the roses from off the top of the coffin. When she opened the upper half of the coffin, she found her father lying in it peacefully, hands interlocked at his waist. "Come on, daddy, let's go home!" she opened up the second half of the coffin. Right then, Jabar grabbed her by her wrist, halting her actions.

"He's dead, ma, he's long gone. Now come on, let's..." Jabar's words were cut short. A scowling Yada spun around and smacked the dog shit out of him, bloodying his mouth. With wide eyes and an opened mouth, he felt around inside of his grill with his tongue. He tasted the blood inside of his mouth which tasted like metal and spat on the ground. Jabar wanted to ring Yada's neck, but his understanding of her grieving gave her a pass.

"No! Don't chu say that! Don't chu say that to me! My daddy is not dead! He's alive, and he's coming home with me, now!" Yada roared harshly seemingly having gone mad. She then turned back around to her father's coffin, grabbing his hand and trying to take him out of the coffin. At this time, half of the funeral attendants began breaking off to get a hold on the situation. Yada had slipped her arms under her dead father's arms and was pulling him out little by little.

"Jesus, she's trying to take him outta the coffin," a man said. He was shocked. He couldn't believe what was going on before his eyes.

"Oh, my God! Somebody stop her!" a woman called out hysterically.

"Daddy, please, get up! Yo baby girl needs you! I need you!" Yada sobbed and the tears continued to pour down her cheeks, splashing on the ground below.

"Oh my God, Yada!" Tears came bursting out of LeLe's eyes from behind her oversized designer shades. She placed her hands over the lower half of her face and sobbed aloud, body shaking hard with grief. Seeing her best friend in her current state of sadness and turmoil really fucked with her soul. The death of her father was a tragedy that she suffered great heartache from, and she'd probably never ever be the same again after the funeral. Of all their years of being friends, LeLe had never seen her girl like this. The entire scene seemed so surreal. "Yada, calm down! Calm down!" gathering herself as best as she could, LeLe ran towards Yada with the other attendants with hopes of restraining her.

Bang tried to grab Yada and she swung on his ass. He ducked the wild swing and grabbed her arm. Someone else grabbed her other arm. She mad dogged him and kicked him in the nuts; he doubled over, grabbing his privates. That's when Bang grabbed her other arm. Another dude came from behind Yada and grabbed her legs, hoisting her up.

"Get the fuck off of me! You don't know what you're talking about. He's still alive! He's still alive goddamn it! Let me go! I'll kill you, I'll fucking kill you all!" Yada jerked and turned her body, trying her damndest to break free from the men's steel-like grips. No matter how hard she tried to get loose, their grips weren't coming undone. Realizing that her struggling was futile, Yada went limp in her captors' arms. Her head dropped, leaving her hair dangling above ground. She cried and cried about her father's death, tears cascading down her cheeks. Yada's chest quaked and her head bobbed. Little mama's heart was broken beyond repair. Her soul was aching. She was blinded by grief. Her father's death was the equivalent to taking a machete to the chest. The saddest part about it was, she was hurting so bad, that she believed there wasn't anything in the whole, wide world that could heal her pain.

That night

Yada and LeLe got shit-faced at the repast. When they got back home, LeLe had called it quits and decided to go to bed, while Yada popped a bottle of champagne and kept the party going. Jabar tried to get her to ease off the bottle several times, but he failed miserably. You see, Yada wasn't trying to hear anything that he had to say. She wanted to get drunk out of her mind so she wouldn't have to deal with the reality of her father being dead.

Yada had gotten through half of the expensive champagne when she started throwing up like a sick ass dog. Dropping the champagne bottle, she dashed to the bathroom, leaving vomit droppings in her wake. Jabar was right on her heels. He made it to the bathroom just in time to see her drop to her knees and open the commode's lid, hurling inside of the bowl. Seeing that her hair was getting in the way of the task at hand, Jabar walked into the bathroom and stood over her. He gathered her hair into a ponytail and held on as she continued to throw up the contents of her stomach. Yada threw up until she was dry heaving. Once she was done, she sat back, leaning against the bathroom sink. Her eyes were glassy, and her mouth was wet, and ropes of saliva and mucus hung from her chin.

"You good, ma?" Jabar asked as he tied a scrunchie around her ponytail that he'd found on the bathroom sink.

"I think—I think I'll be fine," Yada sniffled and wiped her chin with the back of her hand.

"Cool. Well, look, I'ma mop up that mess you made. Then I'ma go to yo room and grab you some underwear and something to slip on. You got vomit all over yo shirt and the side of yo neck. Ok?" he looked at her with his hand on her shoulder. She nodded yes to his question. Afterwards, he shot her a grin and headed out of the bathroom to do what he'd told her he was going to do.

Jabar mopped up the vomit and champagne on the floor. By the time he came back to the bathroom, he found Yada lying in the same spot that he'd left her. He had a black silk pajama set with her initials sewn on the breast pocket, a bra and panties hanging over his arm. He placed them all on top of the big and small towel which was hanging on the rack.

"Come on, lil' lady, let's get chu cleaned up." Jabar told Yada, pulling her up to her feet. He then pulled a black garbage bag from out of his right back pocket and opened it at her feet, standing back upright. "Look, I ain't trying nothing. I'ma help you peel off these dirty clothes and put 'em in that bag. Then I'ma help you get undressed so you can hop in the shower, cool?"

"Unh huh," Yada said as she rocked back and forth on wobbly legs, stink drunk. She smelled like vomit and alcohol, but this didn't seem to offend Jabar. Yada looked down at her clothing as Jabar undressed her. She then looked up at his face. He looked up at her as he carried on the task, grinning. She smiled. "You wanna fuck me, don't chu, Jabar?"

Jabar chuckled and said, "What makes you say that?"

"Nigga, don't try to front. I see how yo ass be looking at me," She said seriously. "I know yo ol' ugly ass dying to bury yo face up in this pussy. Now tell me that I'm lying." Jabar remained silent and continued with his removal of Yada's clothing. "That's what the fuck I thought. I been knew you liked me though. I wasn't fucking witchu though."

"Oh, yeah? Why is that?" he helped her pull her top off and then he dropped it inside of the black garbage bag at Yada's feet.

"To keep it one-hundred witchu, babe, I like them pretty boy thug type of niggaz. Them, them..."

"Them Voss type of niggaz." Jabar said frowning up. The very mention of that nigga Voss's name got his blood to boiling.

Yada snapped her fingers and pointed at him, saying, "Bingo. I love that type of nigga. I can't lie though. I'm off that alcohol and you looking fine than a mothafucka right now, on my daddy."

"I hear you, slim." Jabar removed her skirt and dropped it inside the bag. Next, he helped her take off her bra and panties, dropping them both inside of the bag. Afterwards, he tied up the black garbage bag and placed it by the bathroom door. When he turned back around, he saw Yada on her feet, butt ass naked, nodding like a dope fiend. Jabar took his time to admire her banging ass body. She had it going on. Little mama was strapped from front to back. "Damn, my nigga, I'd bang that shit out the frame." He bit down on his bottom lip as he grasped the bulge in his jeans, raping Yada with his eyes. Snapping himself out of it, Jabar went ahead to get the water going so she could take a shower.

He turned the dials of the shower, adjusting the temperature of the water to the way he liked it. He stuck his hand into the spraying water to make sure that it was just right.

He then flicked his fingers, sending excess water flying from his hand. Next, Jabar grabbed Yada by her hand and walked her over to the tub. By this time, she was coming back to what was going on around her. Jabar helped Yada step inside of the tub and into the spray of hot water.

Once Yada was inside of the tub, she placed her hands on the wall and bowed her head, letting the water beat down on her head and shoulders. While she was doing this, Jabar was lathering her with a loofah and Dove body wash. After he washed her up, he washed her hair. Once he was done, Yada told him to give her a minute alone. Once he had gone, she let the water wash over her body, using the showers soothing liquid as therapy. The hot water released the tension from her body and put her a little at ease. But it couldn't stop the tears that eventually came spilling down her cheeks.

Yada's tears mixed in with the water that sprayed from the showerhead. At that moment, Jabar ran into the bathroom. He turned off the dials and took Yada by her hand, helping her out of the tub one foot at a time. He snatched the towel off the rack, and when he turned around Yada was throwing herself into him, wrapping her arms around his neck. He was stunned at first, but seeing how emotional she was, he succumbed to embracing her.

"Shhhhh, everything is gonna be ok. I promise. I got cho back." Jabar held her in his arms, rubbing her back, affectionately. Her wet body soaked into his shirt, but he didn't pay it any mind.

Dripping wet, Yada cried in Jabar's arms, until she couldn't cry any more. She then looked up at Jabar with a tear streaked face, kissing him. Jabar kissed her back, sticking his tongue inside of her mouth. 'Mmmmm' sounds began to fill the bathroom as Yada and Jabar made out, turning their heads counter clockwise. Jabar grabbed her by her meaty buttocks and squeezed firmly.

While they were making out, Yada unbuckled Jabar's belt and unzipped his pants. She pulled his boxers down and grabbed his long, thick dick. She stroked his shit up and down, causing pre-cum to ooze out of its head.

While all of this was going on, the bathroom grew hot and a fog gradually formed.

Jabar shut his eyelids and threw his head back, mouth hanging open. "Shiiiiiit! That feels good, babe, that feels reallllll good." He licked his lips and bit down on his bottom one, enjoying the sensational feeling that Yada's hand brought him. While she was jerking his meat, Yada sucked on Jabar's neck and bit on his chin softly. She then stuck her tongue inside of his mouth and he began sucking on it. They then started kissing long and hard, saliva smacking around inside of their mouths. "I want—I want some of this pussy, baby," Jabar said as he fingered Yada's soaking wet pussy, making her drip on the floor between her bare feet.

"Uhhhh, uhhhh, uhhhh!" Yada threw her head back, eyes white, mouth open, body jutting as Jabar's fingers went in and out of her. He thrust his fingers between her legs, using them like a dick.

"Can I have some of it, huh? Can a nigga get some of this pussy, baby?" Jabar asked Yada as he stared down into the pleasure etched across her face. Seeing that she was pleased made his dick get harder. A clear liquid leaked out of his pee hole and dripped out of the tip of his dick head.

"Yes—yes—you can get this pussy." Yada gave in to his will. Roughly, Jabar turned her around and forced her up against the wall. He kicked her legs apart and bent her over, hiking her ass up in the air, making it look like a big ass caramel heart.

Damn!

Jabar feasted his eyes on the gooey, wet opening of Yada's pussy. He licked his lips and tapped his dick against her left buttocks, making a smacking sound against it. While he was doing this, the side of Yada's face and hands were pressed against the wall. Yada's eyelids were squeezed shut and her mouth was hanging open in anticipation of feeling Jabar's rock-hard dick deep inside of her tight wet pussy.

Yada peeled her eyelids open and looked at her reflection in the mirror. She saw Jabar behind her, holding his dick, moving to enter her womanhood. Her eyes doubled in size when she saw Voss in the fog, watching them about to get it in. She squeezed her eyelids shut again, and then peeled them back open. Voss had vanished. Right then, she sobered up and stood upright, turning to Jabar. "I'm sorry, but I can't do this. I just can't." she grabbed him under his arm.

"What? What's the matter? What's wrong?" Jabar asked with a furrowed forehead. He was anticipating getting some of that pussy. He was so close he could reach out and touch it, and before he knew it the shit was being snatched out of his sight. Fuck!

Yada ushered Jabar out of the bedroom as he was pulling up his pants and buckling his belt. She slammed the door shut behind him and locked it. Placing her back against the door, she slid down to the floor, with her knees up at her chest. She rested her forearms at the top of her knees and bowed her head, crying. Big teardrops fell, splashing on the tiled floor.

Yada was so hurt and confused. She couldn't understand why she still had feelings for Voss after he had murdered her father. The way she saw it she shouldn't have felt shit about fucking Jabar with how dirty Voss had done her family. But she couldn't help that she still had feelings for him. She knew that it was something that she was going to have to get over—in time. No amount of weed, alcohol or sex was going to help her get over her lover or his betrayal.

It was something that was just going to come naturally. She couldn't speed up the process no matter how hard she tried. It was how it was.

***

Yada lie under her salmon pink silk sheets in bed, the side of her face pressed against her tear soaked pillow as she cried her eyes out in the dark. She couldn't believe that her father was murdered. And she couldn't wrap her head around the fact that it was her husband that had killed him. Yada didn't get it. How can someone that claimed to have loved her so much do something that they knew would hurt her so bad? She was in turmoil. Her heart ached, her soul was shattered, and her body felt weak. Yada wished she could squeeze her eyelids shut, and when she peeled them back open everything would be back to how it was when she'd woken up a week ago. A few times she did just that. But unfortunately, she found herself right where she was. Inside of her bedroom, with the lights off, crying her eyes out.

Knock, knock, knock, knock!

Rapping at the door stole Yada's attention from her grieving. She snatched a few tissues from out of the box of Kleenex sitting beside her canopy bed. Once she used them to dry her eyes and blew her nose, she balled them up and tossed them inside of the waste basket sitting at the side of her bed. Afterwards, she cleared her throat, and looked to the double doors of her master bedroom, responding to her visitor.

"Come in," Yada called out to whomever it was on the other side of the doors. A moment later one of the doors opened and Jabar's silhouette appeared.

"They found 'em, get dressed so we can go." Jabar said before shutting the door closed and walking out of the bedroom. With that having been said, Yada hopped out of bed and hurriedly got dressed so she could confront Voss, and put a bullet in his head for murking her old man. Five minutes flat and she was zipping up her jacket and ready to go. Before leaving, she picked up a portrait of her and her father, which was sitting on the nightstand beside the bed. As tears seeped from out of her eyes, a smile formed on her lips. She swallowed the spit in her throat, wiped her dripping eyes with the back of her hand and kissed the portrait. Once Yada set the portrait back down on the night stand, she left her bedroom, pulling the door shut behind her.

***

Jabar pulled up outside of a white house with a gray rooftop. Its iron fence was scuffed with black marks, but its dying greenish brown lawn was manicured. The house wasn't much to look at. But upon first look you could tell that whomever its owner was kept the property and its surroundings tidy. Well, or at least they tried their best to.

"This is it, get out," Jabar instructed Yada before he jumped out of the car. He then kneeled down and pulled his banga from underneath the driver's seat. Once he recovered his piece, he slammed the driver's door shut and joined up with Yada who was patiently waiting for him on the curb. He nudged her and they entered the yard of the house he and the rest of Lyndell's goons called The House of Pain.

Jabar unlocked the front door of the house and held it open for Yada to enter. Once she did, he came in behind her. He pulled the door shut and locked it behind them. He then led Yada to the basement door, which had a key pad lock beside it, like a safe. Jabar lifted his finger to the key pad, allowing it to linger for a time as he tried to remember the code to it. He then punched in a combination of numbers and the door popped open. As soon as it did he could hear the grunts of a man as he pummeled someone who made pained noises. The sounds of fists pounding wet flesh made Jabar cringe. He knew it was Voss down in the basement and he was taking one hell of a beating.

The way the sound synced in when Jabar had opened the basement door, Yada knew the basement was soundproof. From where she was standing she could also see that the basement's concrete floor was stained burgundy which she assumed may have been blood that had settled and dried. Yada couldn't help wonder what kind of horror stories were behind those blood-stained floors, and if the spirits of the dead haunted the house.

Jabar shut the iron door behind them and slid the huge iron latch across the door, securing it. He then tapped Yada and they made their way down the steps. Along the way they heard the barking of ferocious dogs and niggaz talking mad shit. When they reached the landing of the basement Yada was finally able to see what Voss looked like.

Voss's head was swollen to the size of a pumpkin, his right-eye was swollen shut, and his nose was broken. His face was bloody and sweaty. He was standing on the tips of his sneakers as his wrists were bound together by rope. The rope was hung over a wooden beam in the ceiling and tied to a radiator in the corner. Voss was a bloody mess. From the look of him he appeared to be knocking on death's door. He found himself wincing and wheezing with every breath that he took, feeling like his ribs were broken.

Bang and two goons were standing before Voss. They were all wearing black wife beaters, and their bodies were shiny from perspiration. The goons were holding Uzis as black as their clothing while Bang was warming up Voss's rib cage with punches.

"Ugh!" Voss's body jerked violently as Bang gave him one final punch to the midsection, causing him to spit up blood. The blood splattered on Bang boot and the leg of his cargo pants. He looked down at the nasty glob angrily, then looked up at Voss with hatred in his eyes.

"Bitch ass nigga, you did that shit on purpose!" Bang gave him a three punch combination to the face. Voss's head swung to the left and then dropped down chin touching his chest.

"Woof! Woof! Woof! Woof!"

"Woof! Woof! Woof! Woof!"

The dogs, who were Rottweilers, barked louder and harder, saliva spraying from their mouths.

"Shut cho bitch ass up, nigga!" Bang got angry as fuck; he stormed over to one of the barking hounds and kicked the living shit out of it. The dog howled in pain and cowered in the corner of the basement. Seeing the dog being kicked, the other hound promptly shut the fuck up.

When Yada looked up at Voss and seen how fucked up he was, she couldn't stop the tears from spilling down her cheeks in buckets. She thought for sure she'd lost all of the love she had for him once she found out he was the one that had murdered her father. But seeing him in his current state brought all of her emotions rushing to the forefront for her. Her shoulders trembled like she was freezing cold and she brought her shaky hands to the lower half of her face.

Yada took a deep breath and blew out hot air, wiping her dripping eyes with her fingers. The noise she made caused Bang and the goons to look her way. The goons were about to spray her ass with their Uzis, until it registered to them who she was.

"Fuck you get here, nigga?" Bang asked Jabar as he approached and slapped hands with him.

"Just now. Y'all niggaz slipping, y'all didn't hear our asses come down here?" Jabar said as he looked up at a battered and bruised Voss, dripping blood on the cement floor.

"Hell naw. When lil' mama made that noise my niggaz were about to start blasting."

"You straight, Yada?" Jabar asked her as he swept her hair from out of her face and caressed her cheek with the side of his hand, admiring her beauty. Even when she was crying she was still attractive.

Yada wiped away more of her tears before answering him, saying, "I'll be—I'll be fine. It's just that seeing him brought back up what he'd done to my father. I mean, I—I really loved this nigga and he killed my daddy. Took him away from me," she sniffled and wiped her dripping nose with the back of her hand.

"That's okay, baby. I brought chu here tonight for some get back," Jabar assured her as he rubbed her back soothingly, keeping his eyes on Voss.

Yada turned to Jabar with furrowed brows, wondering what he was getting at. "Get back? Wha—what do you mean?"

Bang looked at Yada like she was retarded or some shit. "Well, damn, lil' mama, you sho is slow. I thought chu were born and bred in the slums."

"Nigga, fallback, she just lost her pops so she's not thinking straight," Jabar took up for Yada and then pulled a pair of black leather gloves from his back pocket, passing them to Yada. She looked at him like she didn't know what to do with them until he told her to put them on. She obliged. He then pulled his gun from the small of his back, holding it up and cocking a flat-head hollow tip bullet into its chamber. Using his gun, he motioned Yada over to him. He stood behind her and placed the gun into her hands, tilting the lethal end of it up toward Voss. "You ready to twist this nigga's cap back for slumping yo old man?"

Yada stared up at Voss with a tear-soaked face, sniffling. She was feeling sorry for him, but then that sorrow turned into hatred. Again, her mind was bombarded by a barrage of the happiest moments of her and her father. Then finally the image of her father lying dead in her arms struck her mind like a bullet. Right then, her eyebrows arched, her nose crinkled and her jaws locked.

Fuck this nigga, Yada! Blast on his ass, he popped yo daddy, just like you said! Took him away from you forever. You can't let that shit slide! Do his punk ass; put a hot one right through his brain!

"Yeahhh, I'm ready," Yada told him confidently.

"Good." Jabar smiled devilishly.

Suddenly, Voss brought his head up. He looked up into Yada's face. His vision was blurry and he was seeing double. He blinked his eyelids a few times and tried his best to focus his sight. Finally, his vision came into focus, and he could clearly see Jabar standing behind Yada with a gun pointed up at him. He opened his mouth to say something and he winded up coughing up blood. He spat blood on the floor and cleared his throat as best he could to speak. He was still hoarse once he could finally say something, but he was sure Yada could hear him though.

"It—it—it wasn't me, baby. I—I didn't kill yo—yo pop—pops," Voss said with a hoarse voice, thick ropes of blood mixed with saliva hanging from his chin. "It was—it was Jabar. Jabar did it."

A furious Jabar came from behind Yada and pointed his finger at Voss, accusingly. "You lying ass bitch! I didn't kill 'em, you peeled the OG, and then shot me! Took my mothafucking ear off!" Jar pointed to the thick bandage that lay over what was left of his war. "Ol' jealous ass mothafucka got mad at Lyndell 'cause he wanted you and me to split the responsibilities of second in command! Emotional ass bitch!" he looked him up and down like he was shit at the bottom of his sneaker, hating the sight of him.

"Fuck you, you fucking faggot! You're the one that's jealous! Jealous of what me and Yada have! Jealous that Lyndell took me under his wing and treated me like a son!"

Voss looked at Yada. "Baby, listen to me, I put that on our love. I put that on our love that I didn't kill yo father!"

Blowl!

Voss slumped where he was hanging, his head bowed, leaving his chin touching his chest. Yada lowered the gun as it wafted with smoke, evaporating in the air.

"That's right, baby girl, handle yo mothafucking business." Jabar told Yada and then looked to Bang. "Check that bitch ass nigga's pulse and see if he's still breathing."

"Fa sho." Bang said as he approached Voss, placing two fingers on the side of his neck. His face frowned up. He looked over his shoulder at Jabar. "This ho ass nigga is still alive, man!"

"Hard to fucking kill," Jabar said under his breath and turned to Yada. "Baby girl, gon' put one in that nigga head, get this shit over with so I can have my niggaz dispose of his body."

"Nah," Yada shook her head, eyes still on Voss, watching his chest slowly rise and fall, as he took short breaths.

"What chu mean, nah? This nigga popped yo goddamn daddy! It's only right that chu get cho revenge for it." Jabar reasoned.

"Fuck this nigga!" Yada spat on the floor and looked back up at Voss. "I want his ass to hang there and bleed to death."

"You mean let 'em suffer?" Jabar asked.

"You goddamn right."

Jabar smiled devilishly and said, "I respect yo gangsta, slim, for real for real." He took the gun away from Yada and stuck it back into the small of his back. "Alright, you got it. We gon' let this bitch nigga bleed to death then we gon' get rid of the body."

Jabar turned to Bang and the goons, telling them what to do with Voss's body once he was officially dead. He then tapped Yada and they made their way toward the staircase. Yada's eyes lingered on Voss. Hot tears stung her eyes and water ran down her cheeks. She then mouthed 'I love you'. With that having been soundlessly said, she turned back around and headed up the staircase.

CHAPTER EIGHT

"Listen, I'ma kick it at cho crib. I don't think it's a good idea that chu be alone tonight." Jabar told Yada from behind the wheel. The street light flickered on and off of them through the windshield, taking them in and out of darkness.

"Oh, you don't have to do that. I'll be fine." Yada assured him.

"Nah. I'ma take care of you. I know that's what OG would want me to do. And I don't mind."

"Well, if you insist." Yada focused her attention out of the passenger window, watching the street fly past her.

***

When Yada and Jabar came through the door of her mansion, she heard a noise that stole her attention. Her brows crinkled and she looked at Jabar, who was rubbing his stomach.

"Nigga, you farted?" Yada asked seriously covering her nose and mouth.

"Nah, that was my stomach growling. I'm hungrier than a bitch. You think you can hook a nigga up witta sandwich or something?" Jabar inquired as he walked towards the living room.

"Yeah, just limme use the bathroom right quick. Make yo self at home." She watched Jabar flop down on the living room couch and grab the remote control, flipping on the television set.

Yada headed upstairs where she raised the commode's lid, pretending to take a piss. She then turned on the faucet water, allowing the water to flow as she searched the medicine cabinet for a bottle of Benadryl. She took the capsules down and stashed them inside of her pocket. She then cut the water off and headed back downstairs, passing by Jabar as she headed inside of the kitchen. Jabar licked his lips and grabbed the bulge in his jeans watching her bodacious ass bounce from left to right. He then focused his eyes back on the flat screen TV.

"What kinda sandwich do you want?" Yada asked right before she disappeared through the doorway.

"Salami, please," he responded, "Extra mayo, lettuce, pickles, onions and tomatoes, oh, and mustard."

Yada went inside of the refrigerator and took out all of the items she'd need to prepare Jabar a salami sandwich. She then grabbed the loaf of bread from out of the pantry. As she went along with making Jabar's sandwich, she called out to him.

"Aye, what do ya want to drink?" Yada's voice rang out inside of the living room.

"A Heineken, if you got one." Jabar responded.

"Hold up," she held the refrigerator door open as she looked through the shelves, finding the beer he desired. "Yeah, we got Heineken."

"Cool." She heard him respond.

Yada finished making the sandwich and sucked the mayo off of her thumb. She put the items she'd used away, and grabbed the Heineken. She took the bottle-opener out of the kitchen drawer and popped the top on it. She then looked back and forth between the bottle of beer and the kitchen door, opening the Benadryl capsules and dumping their contents inside of the bottle. Once she was done, she discarded the capsules and placed the sandwich on a plate along with a few cheese and cheddar potato chips. Picking the plate up, Yada made her way inside of the living room where she saw Jabar on his cellular, its screen shining on his face.

"Dinner is served," Yada entered the room with a smile on her face, sitting the plate and beer down on the coffee table before him.

"Thank you," Jabar sat his cell phone down and pigged out on the food. Yada watched him stuff his face for a moment before she left the room. She returned an hour later to find Jabar's ugly ass slumped on the couch, snoring like a mothafucka, with his mouth wide open.

"Sleeping Beauty," Yada said before she headed back upstairs, and inside of her bedroom. She strapped on a Kevlar bulletproof vest, threw on a hoodie, gloves, tied a black bandana around her neck and grabbed her .45 automatic handgun from underneath the mattress. Gripping it with both hands, she pointed it at something imaginary across the bedroom, taking aim. Satisfied with her gun of choice, she tucked it into the small of her back. She then grabbed her cell phone and dialed up LeLe who was out doing God only knows what, telling her where to meet her. Once she disconnected the call, she made her way out of the mansion and into the night where she jumped inside of the passenger seat of Dough Boy's car.

***

Bang and the goons kicked it on the front porch of The House of Pain, waiting for that nigga Voss to die off. They shot the shit while passing a smoldering blunt between them. Bang had just hit the bleezy and passed it to one of the goons, when his cellular suddenly rung. Reaching into his pocket, he pulled it out and looked at its screen. B.M. was on the display.

"Shit!" Bang said staring at the cell phone's screen, blowing smoke out of his nostrils and mouth.

"What's up, bro?" one of the goons asked holding smoke in his lungs before blowing it out in a cloud.

"It's my baby momma. I was supposed to slide out with her crazy ass to her mother's birthday party. I know this bitch ain't doing nothing but calling to cuss my ass out, and

I don't feel like hearing that shit. I already know she gon' keep banging my line until I pick it up though so I may as well face the fucking music. Y'all niggaz be quiet for a second, man."

"Alright." The goon responded before passing the blunt to the other.

"'Sup?" Bang spoke into the cellular. His brows furrowed and his eyes shifted back and forth as he listened to what was being told to him. "Junior? How the fuck did that happen? Shiiiit. What hospital they taking 'em to? Ok. I'll see you up there." He disconnected the call and turned to the goons. "Look, y'all, I gotta go. Some shit came up with my son. Once that nigga down there is dead, y'all get rid of the body." Bang ran from off the porch, hopped the fence with one hand over to the sidewalk and ran across the street. He opened the door to his Charger, hopped in behind the wheel, and peeled off. The wheels of his tires screeched as he busted a U-turn in the middle of the street and sped off in the opposite direction.

"Yo, you think that nigga baby momma really called 'em, or was he frontin' so he could get outta helpin' us get rid of homeboy's body?" the goon said, cupping his hand around the half smoked blunt hanging from his mouth and lighting it again. He sucked on the end of the blunt and blew out a cloud of smoke.

"Somebody called 'em, but I doubt it was about his fucking kid. I'm witchu. That nigga just didn't wanna help us with this goddamn body. Sorry ass motha—" the goon was cut short when his dome suddenly exploded, and his brain splattered against the house. He fell over the banister and landed hard on his back with a thud.

When the other goon saw his homeboy fall over the banister, his eyes grew big and he looked around for where the bullet had come from. He couldn't identity where the shot was fired from so he reached for the newspaper, which was covering his Uzi. He'd just snatched the newspaper from off his weapon, when the side of his skull exploded. His brain fragments went up in the air and rained down to the floor. The goon's body hit the surface, and right after came his blunt with its ember burning.

As soon as the last goon was laid out dead, there was ruffling in the bushes on either side of the house. Suddenly, Dough Boy arose from the left bushes, gloved hand holding a Glock with a silencer on its barrel. His menacing eyes were peering out of the holes of a burgundy ski mask. He made his way up the steps and onto the porch. He moved to each goon, kicking them in their side and watching them, to see if they'd move. They stayed still. At that moment, Yada emerged with a .45 automatic handgun with a silencer on its barrel. She was wearing a blue bandana over her head and over the lower half of her mouth. Her eyes were hidden behind black sunglasses.

She'd taken out the second goon while that nigga Dough Boy had laid down the first goon.

Yada motioned for Dough Boy to follow her as she opened the front door of the house. She moved inside of the house like a police officer, swaying her .45 from left to right. Once she figured out the upstairs was clear, she moved toward the basement door.

Dough Boy had gotten out of the penitentiary a few weeks before Voss had gotten out. Voss had made sure his main man had some paper in his pocket and a place of his own to call home.

"Stand back, I got this!" Dough Boy told her, and went to aim his Glock at the key pad's lock. He thought he was going to fire a shot at the goddamn thing and it was going to short circuit. That way the iron door would open, and they could make their way inside. The nigga watched way too many movies!

"Hold up!" Yada outstretched her hand and motioned for him to lower his gun. "I think I remember the code for it," She looked at the floor, looking like she was in deep thought. Once she figured that she had recalled the combination that Jabar had punched in, she stepped to the key pad and punched in the number. The door beeped and flashed red. The combination was wrong. She tried again. Still didn't work. "Fuck, fuck, fuck!"

"Come on now! We gotta go! There are two dead bodies outside. Ain't no telling who seen what, and are going to blow the whistle to The Ones." Dough Boy told her. He was looking over his shoulder every five seconds, impatiently bouncing from foot to foot.

"Hold the fuck on!" Yada kept her eyes cast to the floor as she tried to recall the code again. Figuring that she remembered the combination that Jabar had entered, Yada punched in the number. The door beeped and flashed green. The iron door popped open.

Yada pulled open the door. Holding her gun with both hands, she crept down the staircase, carefully. Dough Boy was right behind her, gripping his shit up with both hands, creeping down the steps just like she was. When they made it down to the landing of the basement, they saw the Rottweilers licking Voss's blood up from the cement floor. Yada moved in, swaying her .45 from left to right, nozzle spitting flames. The dogs yelped painfully and fell out dead, holes in their skulls.

"We're here, baby! Me and Dough Boy! Hold on we're gonna get chu outta here!" Yada tucked her warm gun into the small of her back and pulled the blue bandana down from the lower half of her face. "Dough Boy, you grab 'em,

I'ma cut 'em down." She told her counterpart and unsheathed the bowie knife from her side. As she approached the end of the rope to cut her man down, Dough Boy looked around the basement until he found a blanket. He flapped it out and made his way toward Voss.

Yada waited by the radiator with the knife in her hand. Once she saw that Dough Boy was prepared to grab Voss before he hit the floor, she chopped the rope twice. The rope gave on the second swing, and Dough Boy caught Voss before he could hit the cement floor, covering him up with the blanket. The first thing he did was look at the gun-shot wound in Voss's torso, which was on the right side, away from his vital organs.

"Good, good. You didn't hit anything that would have killed him instantly." Dough Boy announced to Yada. She walked over to them and placed her fingers on his neck, checking his pulse. Voss's eyes were rolled into the back of his head and his mouth was slightly peeled open. He was moaning, and in great pain, but he was still alive.

"Thank God. We've gotta hurry up so you can get 'em to the hospital. Come on." Yada pulled the blue bandana back up over the lower half of her face and pulled out her .45. She made her way back up the staircase, gun leading the way, and Dough Boy on her heels carrying Voss.

Yada and Dough Boy made hurried footsteps out of the yard and down the sidewalk, heading toward Dough Boy's Easter Bunny white Denali. Yada tucked her gun at the small of her back and pulled open the passenger door. She moved aside and let Dough Boy sit Voss down in the seat. He then ran over to the driver's door and jumped in behind the wheel, slamming the door shut behind him.

Yada pressed her finger against the ear bud in her ear and spoke. "Le, pull up, we're at Dough Boy's truck." At that moment, LeLe sped up the block and stopped, tires screeching. Yada peered over the windshield of the Denali. She held up one finger, signaling for LeLe to give her one minute. She wanted a moment with Voss before he was driven away.

"Baby, baby, baby," Yada called for Voss's attention but he didn't answer. He moaned and groaned. That's when she cupped his face and looked into his eyes. His pupil was moving around aimlessly, and he was still moaning. "Baby, focus, look at me," She sniffled, tears threatening to spill from out of her eyes.

Voss eyes focused on Yada's tear streaked face. "Yada, is that—is that really you, baby?" He asked weakly. His left eye was swollen shut. He could see through his right eye, but his vision was tinted red from blood running into it. He continuously blinked it trying to keep more blood from getting into it.

"Oh, yes, yes, baby, it's me!" she sniffled again and tears slowly spilled down her cheeks. "Oh, my God, Voss, I love you. I love you so much, baby."

"Why—why did you shoot me, then?"

"I'm sorry, baby. I'm so, so sorry. But I had to in order to get Jabar to believe I wanted you dead. But everything is going to be ok, 'cause Dough Boy is going to see to it that chu get to the hospital. Ok?"

"O—okay."

"Baby, listen, I'm going to ask you something, and I need to know the truth. Can you do that? Can you tell me the truth, no matter what it is?" he nodded yes. "Baby, did you...did you kill my father?" Yada watched to see if his right-eye would twitch when he answered. But he didn't say anything and his eye didn't move. He was too busy moaning in pain.

"Hos—hospital," Voss croaked, wincing.

"Look, ma, that's a question better asked at another time. Right now, I need to get 'em to a hospital, ASAP."

"Ok." Yada nodded rapidly. She wiped her teardrops away. "Dough Boy is going to take you to the hospital now. You hang on, you just hang on 'til you get there and get some help." She kissed him tenderly on the lips. She then turned to the passenger window, fogging it up with her hot breath. A fresh set of tears pooled in her eyes, obscuring her vision. Using her finger, she wrote *I Love You.* Voss watched as the fog cleared up and the words disappeared.

Yada kissed Voss again. She then slammed the door shut behind her, and ran over to LeLe car. She jumped into the passenger seat and slammed the door shut. As soon as she did, LeLe pulled off heading into one direction while Dough Boy went in the other.

"Is Voss going to be ok?" LeLe asked, glancing back and forth between the windshield and Yada.

"I don't know…God I don't know. But I hope so 'cause if not, I'll die. I know I'll die 'cause it will be all my fault." Yada's voice became shaky and cracked under her raw emotions. She broke down, slobbering and crying, hands pressed against her face. Yada didn't know for sure if Voss was going to make it to the hospital on time or not but she was going to beg and plead with God to spare his life, even if it meant taking hers so that he could live. Little mama had already lost her mother and father, so if she was to lose the only man she'd ever truly loved, she'd go insane. Her heart would shatter into a million pieces, and her soul would quake. The loss of Voss Purdy would definitely be a loss that she could not take.

LeLe glanced back and forth between the windshield and Yada. She then pulled Yada under her arm, hugging her against the side of her body. "Shhhhh, shhhhh, everything is going to be all right, momma. Voss is going to make it to the hospital. You just watch and see. God's got 'em." LeLe kissed the top of Yada's head as she continued to rub her arm, sympathetically. Yada continued to cry her eyes out, as they drove along.

***

Dough Boy looked back and forth between the windshield and Voss, making sure he was still breathing.

"You good, my nigga?" Dough Boy questioned with concern.

"Yea—yeah, I'll be fine," Voss said, with his attention focused out of the passenger window. He was thinking about the note Yada left behind. "Roll the windows up and turn the heat on for me," He told him weakly. Dough Boy rolled up the window is his truck, and cut on the heater. A minute later the note that Yada had written on the passenger window appeared, I Love You. A slight smirk formed on Voss's lips as he stared at the message. Dough Boy glanced over at him to see what he'd had in mind to do. He watched as he wrote with his finger, too. As in *I Love You, Too.* He then envisioned Yada's face before his eyes, smiling at him as she stared at him admiringly. He smiled back at her.

***

LeLe pulled up in the driveway of Yada's mansion and slaughtered the engine.

Yada turned to LeLe and said, "Thanks for always having my back, girl."

LeLe waved her off like it wasn't a big deal and countered. "Don't even mention it, girl. You know you my nigga, and I'd do anything for you. And vice versa. You know how we do."

"You my bitch forever," Yada said, swearing her allegiance to their friendship.

"Forever and a day, momma," She hugged Yada affectionately, and kissed her on the cheek.

The girls then hopped out of the car. LeLe went on up the steps while Yada pulled her hood down over her head and tucked her hands inside of her hoodie, walking up the steps behind her. Pulling out her keys, Yada pressed her ear against the front door and listened closely. Little mama felt like she'd given Jabar enough Benadryl, to put him out for a while. But she could never be too sure. When she didn't hear anything besides the television playing inside of the living room, she unlocked the door and she and LeLe stepped inside. Yada shut the door behind them quietly, locking it. The girls hugged one another once again, before LeLe made her departure upstairs.

Yada turned her attention to the living room. She could see the top of Jabar's head standing where she was, at the door. From the way he was slumped on the couch, she knew his ass was asleep. Placing her keys inside of her pocket, she slowly walked inside of the living room. Coming upon Jabar, she saw that he was indeed asleep. His glass of juice was empty and sitting on the coffee table next to his plate of half eaten tuna sandwich. Homie was snoring loud. He suddenly made an ugly face, dug in his nose and then farted.

"I don't know if you killed my daddy or not. But if I find out you did, that's gon' be yo ass, nigga." Yada scowled. She then made her hand into the shape of a gun and pointed it at Jabar, pretending to shoot him dead. The light from the flat screen television danced across the upper half of her body. Her eyes lingered on him for a moment longer, before she made her way upstairs to her bedroom.

***

Boom!
The double doors of the emergency ward flew open. The hospital staff rushed Voss along on a gurney, tearing open his shirt and exposing the black bleeding hole in his torso. His eyes were hooded, and his pupils moved around

lazily. He tried to say something and winded up coughing up blood.

"Hold on, my nigga, Hold on!" a teary eyed Dough Boy told Voss, running alongside the gurney, clutching his hand. Dough Boy tried to maintain his G, but seeing his homie all fucked up like that caused the tears to fall and drench his face. Once they started it was like he couldn't stop them from falling.

"Sir, I'm going to need you to let him go. We'll take care of him from here," one of the doctors told Dough Boy. The big homie wasn't trying to hear him though. His main concern was the condition that his right-hand man was in.

Voss's eyes became glassy with tears as he stared up at the ceiling. He could see angels in all white flying back and forth across the ceiling, playing violins and smiling at him, flapping their long feathery wings. They were shining brightly and had an eerie mystique to them. Voss didn't know what it was but them being there brought a sense of comfort to him. As funny as it may seemed, giving his current circumstances, their presence made him feel as if everything was going to be fine.

Dough Boy's face balled up, because it seemed as if Voss was looking at something. He looked where Voss's line of vision ended and didn't find anything there. Then, that's when it came to Dough Boy that he was probably looking up at an angel or a deceased loved one.

"Nah, Blood, you can't go with them! You gotta stay here with us! Stay here with us, dawg!" Dough Boy urged him, tears bursting out of his eyes. Dough Boy pulled a burgundy bandana from out of his right back pocket and tied it around Voss's right wrist. Voss didn't take his eyes off the angels flying in circles above his head. A smile spread across his lips, and tears of joy spilled down his cheeks.

"I'm sorry, sir, but you've gotta go. We've gotta do our job," the doctor that had spoken to Dough Boy earlier said, pulling his hand free from Voss's hand. Slowly, Dough Boy's palm and fingers released his hand. Right then, another doctor looped an oxygen mask over his nose and mouth. Inside of the mask fogged with each weak breath that he took, lungs inflating and deflating.

Standing where she was inside of the hallway, Dough Boy saluted Voss with the Blood gang sign.

"Stay strong, Blood! Stay strong!"

Dough Boy's words echoed throughout the hallway as he stood where he was, watching the hospital staff rush Voss into emergency surgery. Standing where he was inside of the corridor, Dough Boy watched the gurney and the hospital staff become as small as ants before his eyes.

***

Jabar lie slumped on the couch still fast asleep. The sun's rays shined through the window and kissed off of his face. There was knocking at the door which grew louder and louder, the longer it took for someone to answer it. "I'm coming!" Yada called out as she reached the front door, coming from downstairs.

Knock, knock, knock, knock!

"I said 'hold the fuck on!" Yada called out again. The knocking stopped as she reached the door. She peered out of the window, recognizing who it was at her front door. Her brows furrowed with surprise. She then went on and unlocked the door, pulling it open. As soon as she pulled the door back, Bang walked inside of her house with a couple of goons bringing up the rear. He had a dead serious expression on his face and didn't bother to speak, which Yada felt was rude, considering he was entering her home.

"Well, hello, to you too, Bang," Yada tightened her robe on her and shut the front door, locking it back. Once she did, she entered the living room along with everyone else to see what was going on.

"Yo, wake up, wake up!" Bang called out to Jabar, but he wasn't waking up. "I said 'wake yo punk ass up, nigga!" he kicked the hell out of the couch which finally woke Jabar up.

A frowning Jabar stirred awake looking at Bang like he was crazy. He actually had the thought of picking up his gun, which was lying on the side of him beneath a pillow and shooting his mothafucking ass for breaking his sleep. The only reason why he didn't was because he figured if he was there then it had to have been very important. He had told the nigga where he was at and to hit him up if he needed him, but he'd decided to drop by instead.

Jabar sat up on the couch, stretching his arms and yawning, looking around at all of the goons surrounding him. All of them niggaz were wearing dead serious expressions and looked like they were ready to bring it to niggaz that violated. That's exactly why that nigga Lyndell had them on his payroll. They were a bunch of head hunting niggaz from different hoods all over Southern California.

"Fuck you want? Can't chu see I was getting my beauty sleep?" Jabar picked up his pack of Newports, taking out a cigarette and sparking it up. He tossed the pack back on the table, sucked on the end of the square and blew out a big ass cloud of smoke. He then scratched his temple with his thumb, giving Bang his undivided attention.

"Jerome and Titty are dead! Niggaz hit the spot and snatched up Voss!" Bang informed him regretfully.

"What the fuck you mean?" Jabar frowned up and shot to his feet, blowing smoke from his nose and mouth. "If they dead, how the fuck is yo black ass still alive?"

Bang explained to Jabar the emergency that came up that called for his immediate attention. With the report having been given to him, Jabar nodded, understanding the urgency.

"This shit was an inside job. All the niggaz that knew where we were taking that nigga were in-house." Jabar told him.

"You bet cho nut sack it is, and we're about to find out who did it, too." Bang assured him.

"How?" Jabar's forehead creased with curiosity.

Bang twisted his lips and shook his head, looking at Jabar like he was an imbecile. "The surveillance cameras we had installed you forgetful mothafucka! I got the tape right here." He held up the VHS tape to the surveillance cameras.

Yada's eyes widened when she saw Bang hold up the video tape. She sunk further in the background, moving toward the front door. She took a step back and bumped into someone. She turned around and found one of the goons behind her. When she looked around, she noticed she was surrounded by goons. Them niggaz had her closed in, and there wasn't any way she could get out.

"Excuse me," Yada said to the goon, but he didn't say shit back. She turned back around and stuck her hand inside of her robe, gripping her gun. If shit went left then she was going to blast her way up out that bitch!

Jabar smiled evilly and took the tape from Bang, saying, "Whoever in this room busted homie outta that house is a dead man! I don't give a fuck who it is! Bang, guard the door, I'ma 'bouta put the tape in." With that having been said, Jabar approached the DVD/VHS player to put the tape in.

Bang brushed past Yada, pulling out his banga so he could stand guard at the front door. Yada glanced over her shoulder and he did just that. When she turned back around

Jabar was popping the surveillance tape into the VCR. The footage showed her and Dough Boy storming the house that Voss was being held hostage in, entering the basement and taking out the Rottweilers. It then showed her about to pull the blue bandana down from her face to reveal her identity. At that moment everybody in the living room, including Jabar, pulled out their guns to execute the traitor.

Oh, shit!

Yada thought as she swallowed the lump of fear in her throat and gripped her gun tighter. She knew then that *that* day may very well be her last day breathing.

To Be Continued...
A GANGSTA'S EMPIRE 2
Coming Soon

Submission Guideline

Submit the first three chapters of your completed manuscript to ldpsubmissions@gmail.com, subject line: Your book's title. The manuscript must be in a .doc file and sent as an attachment. Document should be in Times New Roman, double spaced and in size 12 font. Also, provide your synopsis and full contact information. If sending multiple submissions, they must each be in a separate email.

Have a story but no way to send it electronically? You can still submit to LDP/Ca$h Presents. Send in the first three chapters, written or typed, of your completed manuscript to:

LDP: Submissions Dept
Po Box 870494
Mesquite, Tx 75187

DO NOT send original manuscript. Must be a duplicate.

Provide your synopsis and a cover letter containing your full contact information.

Thanks for considering LDP and Ca$h Presents.

Tranay Adams

A Gangsta's Empire

LIPSTICK KILLAH **III**

Mimi

WHAT BAD BITCHES DO **III**

A HUSTLER'S DECEIT 3

KILL ZONE **II**

By **Aryanna**

THE COST OF LOYALTY **II**

By **Kweli**

SHE FELL IN LOVE WITH A REAL ONE **II**

By **Tamara Butler**

RENEGADE BOYS **III**

By **Meesha**

CORRUPTED BY A GANGSTA **IV**

By **Destiny Skai**

A GANGSTER'S CODE **III**

By **J-Blunt**

KING OF NEW YORK IV

RISE TO POWER III

By **T.J. Edwards**

GORILLAS IN THE BAY II

De'Kari

THE STREETS ARE CALLING II

Duquie Wilson

KINGPIN KILLAZ III

Hood Rich

STEADY MOBBIN' **III**

Marcellus Allen

SINS OF A HUSTLA II

ASAD

TRIGGADALE II

Elijah R. Freeman

MARRIED TO A BOSS II

By Destiny Skai & Chris Green

KINGS OF THE GAME II

Playa Ray

<u>Available Now</u>

<u>RESTRAINING ORDER **I & II**</u>

By **CA$H & Coffee**

<u>LOVE KNOWS NO BOUNDARIES **I II & III**</u>

By **Coffee**

<u>RAISED AS A GOON I, II, III & IV</u>

<u>BRED BY THE SLUMS I, II, III</u>

<u>BLAST FOR ME I & II</u>

<u>ROTTEN TO THE CORE I III</u>

<u>A BRONX TALE I, II</u>

By **Ghost**

<u>LAY IT DOWN **I & II**</u>

<u>LAST OF A DYING BREED</u>

<u>BLOOD STAINS OF A SHOTTA I & II</u>

By **Jamaica**

<u>LOYAL TO THE GAME</u>

<u>LOYAL TO THE GAME II</u>

<u>LOYAL TO THE GAME III</u>

<u>LIFE OF SIN</u>

A Gangsta's Empire

By **TJ & Jelissa**

BLOODY COMMAS I & II

SKI MASK CARTEL I II & III

KING OF NEW YORK I II,III

RISE TO POWER I II

By **T.J. Edwards**

IF LOVING HIM IS WRONG...I & II

LOVE ME EVEN WHEN IT HURTS

By **Jelissa**

WHEN THE STREETS CLAP BACK I & II III

By **Jibril Williams**

A DISTINGUISHED THUG STOLE MY HEART I II & III

LOVE SHOULDN'T HURT I II III

RENEGADE BOYS I & II

By **Meesha**

A GANGSTER'S CODE I &, II III

By J-Blunt

PUSH IT TO THE LIMIT

By **Bre' Hayes**

BLOOD OF A BOSS **I, II, III & IV**

By **Askari**

THE STREETS BLEED MURDER **I, II & III**

THE HEART OF A GANGSTA I II& III

By **Jerry Jackson**

CUM FOR ME

CUM FOR ME 2

CUM FOR ME 3

CUM FOR ME 4

Tranay Adams

An **LDP Erotica Collaboration**
BRIDE OF A HUSTLA **I II & II**
THE FETTI GIRLS **I, II& III**
CORRUPTED BY A GANGSTA I, II & III
By **Destiny Skai**
WHEN A GOOD GIRL GOES BAD
By **Adrienne**
A GANGSTER'S REVENGE **I II III & IV**
THE BOSS MAN'S DAUGHTERS
THE BOSS MAN'S DAUGHTERS II
THE BOSSMAN'S DAUGHTERS III
THE BOSSMAN'S DAUGHTERS IV
THE BOSS MAN'S DAUGHTERS **V**
A SAVAGE LOVE **I & II**
BAE BELONGS TO ME
A HUSTLER'S DECEIT I, II, III
WHAT BAD BITCHES DO I, II
By **Aryanna**
A KINGPIN'S AMBITON
A KINGPIN'S AMBITION **II**
I MURDER FOR THE DOUGH
By **Ambitious**
TRUE SAVAGE
TRUE SAVAGE II
TRUE SAVAGE **III**
TRUE SAVAGE **IV**
TRUE SAVAGE **V**
TRUE SAVAGE **VI**

A Gangsta's Empire

By **Chris Green**

A DOPEBOY'S PRAYER

By **Eddie "Wolf" Lee**

THE KING CARTEL **I, II & III**

By **Frank Gresham**

THESE NIGGAS AIN'T LOYAL **I, II & III**

By **Nikki Tee**

GANGSTA SHYT **I II &III**

By **CATO**

THE ULTIMATE BETRAYAL

By **Phoenix**

BOSS'N UP **I , II & III**

By **Royal Nicole**

I LOVE YOU TO DEATH

By Destiny J

I RIDE FOR MY HITTA

I STILL RIDE FOR MY HITTA

By **Misty Holt**

LOVE & CHASIN' PAPER

By **Qay Crockett**

TO DIE IN VAIN

SINS OF A HUSTLA

By **ASAD**

BROOKLYN HUSTLAZ

By **Boogsy Morina**

BROOKLYN ON LOCK I & II

By **Sonovia**

GANGSTA CITY

Tranay Adams

By **Teddy Duke**

A DRUG KING AND HIS DIAMOND I & II III

A DOPEMAN'S RICHES

HER MAN, MINE'S TOO I, II

CASH MONEY HO'S

By **Nicole Goosby**

TRAPHOUSE KING **I II & III**

KINGPIN KILLAZ

By **Hood Rich**

LIPSTICK KILLAH **I, II**

CRIME OF PASSION I & II

By **Mimi**

STEADY MOBBN' **I, II**

By **Marcellus Allen**

WHO SHOT YA **I, II**

Renta

GORILLAZ IN THE BAY

DE'KARI

TRIGGADALE

Elijah R. Freeman

GOD BLESS THE TRAPPERS I, II, III

THESE SCANDALOUS STREETS I, II, III

FEAR MY GANGSTA I, II, III

THESE STREETS DON'T LOVE NOBODY I, II

BURY ME A G I, II, III, IV, V

A GANGSTA'S EMPIRE I, II, III

Tranay Adams

THE STREETS ARE CALLING

158

Duquie Wilson

MARRIED TO A BOSS...

By Destiny Skai & Chris Green

KINGS OF THE GAME II

Playa Ray

<u>BOOKS BY LDP'S CEO, CA$H</u>

<u>TRUST IN NO MAN</u>

<u>TRUST IN NO MAN 2</u>

<u>TRUST IN NO MAN 3</u>

<u>BONDED BY BLOOD</u>

<u>SHORTY GOT A THUG</u>

<u>THUGS CRY</u>

<u>THUGS CRY 2</u>

<u>THUGS CRY 3</u>

<u>TRUST NO BITCH</u>

<u>TRUST NO BITCH 2</u>

<u>TRUST NO BITCH 3</u>

<u>TIL MY CASKET DROPS</u>

<u>RESTRAINING ORDER</u>

<u>RESTRAINING ORDER 2</u>

<u>IN LOVE WITH A CONVICT</u>

<u>Coming Soon</u>

BONDED BY BLOOD 2

BOW DOWN TO MY GANGSTA

A Gangsta's Empire

www.ingramcontent.com/pod-product-compliance
Lightning Source LLC
Chambersburg PA
CBHW070040260626
47159CB00005B/2091